BUBBLE SCREEN

Books by David Chill

Post Pattern

Fade Route

Bubble Screen

Safety Valve

BUBBLE SCREEN

A Novel By

DAVID CHILL

For Andrea

One

The first time I met Miles Larson, he looked like he wanted to kill someone.

Even though he was clearly over 70 years old and no taller than 5' 8", Miles had the pugnacity of an angry dog whose territory was about to be violated. His wife Clara stood at his side and maintained a similar repose. On the field, the Trojan Marching Band had begun a stirring rendition of "The Star Spangled Banner." The band was spread out sideline-to-sideline on the grassy floor of the Los Angeles Memorial Coliseum, and their formation spelled out the school nickname, T-R-O-J-A-N-S.

"Hey you two!" Miles shouted at a couple in the next row. He then repeated himself until he got their attention. "Take your hats off!"

The young couple were both wearing dark blue baseball caps with italicized lettering that said "Golden Bears." They looked at Miles as if he were from another planet and shook their heads in disgust. Miles' face became contorted with rage at this disregard for what he obviously considered a simple request.

Storming abruptly over to the couple, Miles verbalized his demand once more, this time with his right hand balled up into a fist. While he wasn't a big man, Miles was solidly built and looked like he had some scar tissue on the back of both hands. As the younger man began to ask who he thought he was, Miles shoved a finger two inches from his nose.

"Show some respect for the flag," he yelled.

At that point I sidled over and tried to get in between them. Usually I'm the one to instigate fights rather than prevent them, but Miles was a potential client and keeping him out of trouble suddenly became my first priority.

"I don't think you all want to get thrown out of here," I pointed out to the couple.

"What is this?" the woman protested. "We didn't do anything,"

"Maybe not," I said, wiggling in between Miles and his new friends. "But all of you will get a security escort out of here and you'll miss the game. It's much easier to just take your caps off for 60 seconds."

"It's a free country," the man responded.

"Shut up!" Miles barked. "Now take those damn things off. This is the national anthem!"

I extended my arm to prevent Miles from getting any closer and then turned back to the couple. "You really want to lose these 50-yard line seats? Really? Over this?"

The couple looked at each other in exasperation and then sheepishly removed their headgear. I sensed Miles was about to blurt out a final quip, so before he could make matters worse I grabbed him by the arm and led him back to our seats.

"Damn Cal people," he grumbled. "I'll tell you something, Burnside. I was ready to clock both of them. The girl, too."

"I had a funny feeling about that."

We returned to our seats to enjoy what was left of the national anthem before sitting down. It was a beautiful November afternoon in Los Angeles. Deep blue sky, a few windswept clouds, and a mild 65-degree temperature. A great day to watch a college football game. Not the type of day one wants to ruin by having an altercation over something silly. That is, unless one has an unyielding view of right and wrong.

Miles and Clara Larson were important people at USC. They were important because they had lots of money and gave lavishly to the university. Owners of a successful business for many decades, they were the epitome of the big donors, and were very loyal to the school. They were treated regally, but as Provost Marshall Hunt had warned me earlier in the week, they were loose cannons in many ways.

"There is no filter between their brains and their mouths," he had said. "Especially Miles. He says what's on his mind and thinks anyone who doesn't like it can go take a long walk off a short pier."

"Thanks for making them my problem," I rejoined dryly.

The Provost had laughed heartily. "Oh you'll do well by them, sir. They'll be great clients for you. They believe someone at their company is stealing from them. And when it comes to taking their money, well, that is the ultimate sin.

They view things in very stark, black-and-white terms. The company is called Malco. I made the assumption that with your stellar SC credentials, they'd be eager for your help."

"I appreciate the referral. But if someone's stealing from them, why don't they just go to the police?"

"Oh my, no. They despise anything to do with the government. And they believe the police are tools of the government. They'd rather hire a private investigator. And who better to help them than a former Trojan football star? It didn't hurt that you and Johnny Cleary played together."

It had been over 20 years since I had put on the cardinal and gold uniform, but for some people, my image remained frozen in time. And now that Johnny Cleary had been elevated to head coach of the football team, my status in the Trojan community had only grown. USC had a close knit relationship with its alumni, and maintaining its heritage was very important to the school.

As the band left the field and made way for the teams to line up for the opening kickoff, I turned to Clara. "Does he always get this way?" I asked.

Clara threw her head back and cackled. "Oh sure. He's been tossed out of here a number of times. But he always gets back in once security recognizes who he is."

Having lots of money can help open doors, including the gates at an athletic event. In Los Angeles there were many tiers of wealth, and the Larsons appeared to be somewhere near the upper level. But wealth could be an illusion. The Larsons were not what you would call aristocratic. People who rose to that station in life often employed others to take care of their problems. The Larsons, on the other hand, seemed to delight in a good, old-fashioned confrontation. And Miles had a cantankerous sensibility that was oddly appealing at first, but I imagined it was one that could easily grow stale.

"So Miles," I began. "I understand you have a problem you'd like me to look into."

"I need a snoop," he declared.

"I prefer the term Private Investigator."

"Eh. Call yourself whatever you want, Burnside. I just need someone to go undercover in my warehouse. I'm losing thousands of dollars in product every week."

"I thought you just installed Cable TV systems."

"We do. We're what's called a home service provider. We hook customers up, install the set-top boxes in the homes. But the boxes are starting to disappear like crazy. I know who's doing it, I just can't prove it."

"Have you set up security cameras?"

Miles gave me an incredulous look. "Do I strike you as an idiot? Of course I did. The thieves wore masks and spray-painted the camera lens. I know who it is. I'm having union problems. The shop steward has been a constant thorn in my side during bargaining talks. I'm sure he's behind this."

I sat back for a minute and took all of this in. "You can put in a second set of surveillance cameras. Make them covert. They get activated when the first ones are tampered with. Mount them high up."

Miles thought about this. "That's an idea," he said.

"I understand this is a family business."

"Oh yeah," he nodded. "Peter and Isabelle run the day-to-day. But I'm still the one in charge."

"Your kids work in the business?"

"Yup. Well, two of them, anyway. Got a third kid, the youngest, he decided to move to New York. Works as a consultant on Wall Street. Didn't want to work for his old man, he wouldn't even go to SC. Eddie was always the kid who did things differently."

"Was that disappointing?"

"Eh, it was a long time ago. But in some ways I respect Eddie the most."

"Because he made it on his own."

"Yup. Just like me. Nobody handed me nothing. In fact my old man kicked me out of the house when I was just 18 years old. Forced me to be an adult. I wanted to do that favor for each of my kids. Sink or swim, that's the way. But Clara stopped me."

Clara laughed. "I'm all for being self-sufficient. But you need to help your children get a decent start in life. And sink or swim isn't the best method for everyone. It can lead to a lot of problems down the road."

"Oh heck, Clara, I just wanted to teach them the value of a dollar. My old man used to have me mow his lawn. Paid me 5 cents for a couple hours' work."

"Not a great wage," I said. "No matter what era you grew up in."

"Nope. But I used that nickel each week to buy me a chocolate bar. And it always turned out to be a damn good chocolate bar as a result."

"I didn't think that was the parenting model I wanted to follow," said Clara. "But a child should understand the importance of money, and you do have to earn it."

"So all your kids have successful business careers?" I asked.

"Yeah. They do okay," Miles said. "Maybe not as good as me. But I'm a tough act to follow."

Clara put a hand on my shoulder. "Do you have a family, Burnside?"

I shook my head. "Haven't found the time yet."

She nodded slowly, her helmet of white hair bobbing up and down. While there was a ruddy toughness to her demeanor, she maintained the last traces of what was once a beautiful face. "Found the time for a girlfriend?"

I smiled. "Yes. Gail. In fact she's flying back down here later today. Been interviewing for a job and visiting friends. She just finished law school recently. Up north."

"I'll bet it's tough to have a long distance relationship," Clara said.

"We're used to it," I sighed. "She's been at Berkeley for the last three years."

Miles turned to me with a pained look. "She's been going to school with them socialists?"

I shrugged and didn't respond. Since Miles didn't take kindly to my having a girlfriend who had gone to Cal, I decided not to make things worse by telling him Gail had been an undergraduate at our cross-town rivals in Westwood.

We stopped talking for a moment and stood up to watch the opening kickoff. The game began on a sour note for the Trojans. Cal's kickoff returner caught the ball near the goal line, and began moving up the middle of the field before cutting sharply to the near sideline. Outrunning everyone in the coverage, he scampered untouched all the way into the end zone for a 99-yard touchdown. Within seconds, USC was losing 7-0.

"Bad karma, Miles. You should have let those Cal people wear their caps."

"Heck no," he scowled. "It's un-American. Don't worry. We'll take control of this game soon enough. I have a good feeling about today."

I did too. It had been a few years since I had sat in 50-yard line seats, and it was a treat I wanted to savor. When my old teammate Johnny Cleary was named head coach, he had offered me some sideline passes if I would come in one day and address the team. He wanted to bring back some of the old time Trojan spirit. I told him I would be happy to do it, and with the season winding down, I needed to get back to him soon and keep my promise. As well as working in time for my new client.

"So Miles, I'll stop by your office this week and we can discuss how to approach this."

"Good."

"I just hope we don't get tossed out of the Coliseum today. I'd like to see the end of the game."

"I promise. But I can't vouch for Clara."

"Oh? Has she popped anyone?"

Clara sat back and grinned. "Nope. But I came close last year."

I raised my eyebrows. "You almost got into a brawl?"

Clara gave a devilish smile. "Oh, it wasn't a fight. Last year a couple of young men in the row in front of us decided they wanted to watch the game standing up. I gave one of them a good poke with my umbrella and told them to sit down. They started whining about their rights, too."

Miles chuckled and broke in. "That's when Clara really jammed the umbrella into one of them. Told them if they didn't sit down they wouldn't have any ribs left by halftime."

"I take it they sat down."

"Oh they did. They said they paid hundreds for their seats and I told them we've paid millions to begin the Coliseum renovations. They weren't going to top that."

I doubted many others would either. I looked at Clara. "Glad Miles didn't have to slug anyone."

"I'm glad too," she smiled. "But I think those fellas were more worried about me."

*

The game ended on a high note and Miles' prognostication about today proved correct. USC overcame a seven point deficit at halftime and roared back to beat Cal, 34 to 14. Despite the lopsided score, most fans stayed until the end of the game, causing the usual traffic nightmare exiting the Coliseum area. It took me nearly an hour to navigate the six city blocks from the parking lot to the Harbor Freeway, but once on it, my black Pathfinder hummed down the stretch of asphalt.

Los Angeles International Airport is located on the edge of the Pacific. It's called LAX with the three letters spelled out individually, because that's its three letter airport code. Spotting tourists was easy, as they often pronounce the airport as "Lax," until someone points out they sound like a rube. Traffic was light on a late Saturday afternoon, and I quickly found parking inside the airport. I made my way to the gate at the Southwest Airlines terminal, but discovered Gail's flight from Oakland was delayed a few minutes. I stood inside a bar in the terminal to watch the ESPN highlights of the USC-Cal game I had just come from. Even though I had been at the game, watching the same event on TV always had a different feel to it.

The doors to the gate opened and passengers began exiting the jetway bridge in single file. It took a few minutes, but the love of my life finally walked gracefully into the terminal. She wasn't hard to find. Gail Pepper had dark brown hair that drifted well past her shoulders, pouty lips, and a gleaming smile that could light up a city. She wore jeans and a black turtle-neck sweater. When she saw me approach her, she threw her arms around me and greeted me with a long kiss.

"Hi there, honey," she said."Hope you haven't been waiting long."

"I passed the time thinking of you."

"You're sweet," she smiled. "And you lie a lot."

"Only white lies," I countered. "And I try to use them judiciously."

Gail slipped underneath my right arm, and we walked slowly and contentedly through the terminal and outside into the cool evening air.

"You should be happy," she said, as we walked towards my Pathfinder.

"I am, but is there something in particular you're referring to?"

"USC beat the Bears today."

"Ah. Yes. Good game. I'm surprised you know about it. Football was never one of your passions."

"Still isn't. A group of guys were yelling and screaming in the airport bar before we boarded. They kept complaining, so I imagine Southern Cal was winning."

"You know we prefer to be called USC these days."

"Yes. And I've heard some of your Trojan friends refer to my fellow students as the Dirty Hippies. That was about a century ago."

I smiled. "We do have some diehards. In fact, one of them may become my new client."

Gail seemed intrigued. "I look forward to hearing about that one."

We reached the Pathfinder and I slid her suitcase in the back. As we headed up the San Diego Freeway towards Santa Monica, we argued playfully back and forth on dinner options before agreeing on El Cholo. We were seated quickly and settled in with a pair of margaritas.

"Tell me about your trip," I started.

"Great interview," she said, licking some salt delicately from the rim of the glass. "It would be an amazing opportunity, working on some very high profile cases. The boss is sharp and the money's not bad."

"Any downsides?"

"It's in San Francisco."

"Right. One of our country's most picturesque cities," I pointed out absently and without much conviction.

"I've come to like the Bay Area. ... " she said, her voice trailing off.

"Except?"

"Except you're down here."

I picked up my glass and brushed the salt away with my fingers. Lifting the drink to my mouth, I took a deep swallow. The cold, tangy liquid tasted good.

"I've always been down here," I said.

"And I've missed you for the last three years. I've missed you a lot. Being around you feels good. In fact I plan to use my temporary freedom from work hanging around with you for a while. Your schedule permitting, of course."

"Fine by me," I said. "But aren't there comparable jobs down here in L.A.?"

"I guess. But having spent three years at Berkeley, my contacts are all up in the Bay area. One of my professors is taking a high-level position in that San Francisco office. In fact, that professor recommended me and arranged for the interview."

I felt a bad thought coming on. I tried to keep it inside of me, but I knew it would come out eventually. When you have a girlfriend who looks like Gail, being a little insecure comes with the territory. Better to put the concern on the table now than let it marinate.

"Sounds as if he really likes you," I managed. "And he wants to work closely with you."

"Not exactly what you think."

"You know me and you know where I'm going with this," I said, my imagination starting to move into one of those dark places that feels all too comfortable at times.

"Yes," Gail said, eyeing me closely. "You do tend to assume the worst in everyone."

"Sorry. I'd say it's an occupational hazard but you also know my history."

"Yes, and I wish you'd work on it. You're a good guy who could be a great guy."

"Could be?"

Gail's mouth tightened. "No. You are a great guy. I'm sorry for saying that, I was a little annoyed. And just to set the record straight, yes, my professor likes me and wants to work closely with me. Her name is Hester Goldstein. And she's happily married and has two kids. So you might want to rethink your assumptions."

I smiled to myself and felt the darkness dissipate. "Point taken."

"I do know you well."

I sat back and gazed into those lovely, clear gray eyes. Gail and I had met four years ago and became deeply involved. Instead of taking a toll, the long separation bonded us even more strongly. The time we spent with each other now was special and something we cherished. She had been offered a scholarship to Berkeley Law School, and the opportunity was too good to pass up. We were leading parallel lives in some ways, but still felt very close. I knew that at some point we'd need to make a decision regarding our future. Complacency being what it is, this was a subject more comfortable putting off than in dealing with head on.

"So tell me about your new client," she said.

"I actually may have two clients, but I'll tell you about Miles and Clara first."

"Now *those* names sound like they're from another century."

"Mmm-hmm. So are their attitudes. Miles Larson owns a business, very successful, but he's also incredibly bullheaded and suspicious."

"Seems to go with the territory."

"When you have a lot, you have a lot to lose. He thinks someone at his company is stealing from him. He wants me to go undercover and find out what's happening."

"And then what?"

"And then I have to keep Miles from chopping up the body."

Gail smiled. "This might be a good stretch case for you."

"How so?"

"It might help in your, ahem, mediation skills."

"Are you saying I'm too much of a combatant?"

"Not exactly, honey. In fact one of the reasons I'm drawn to you is because of your tenacity and sense of righteousness."

"But?"

"No buts, *amigo*. I just think you have other talents that could surface."

I sat back and took another long swallow. My usual *modus operandi* was to instigate conflict and then clean up the mess later. By poking and prodding people, I often got them to reveal things they hadn't planned on revealing. Now I was saddled with a client who operated in seemingly the same manner, except getting others to reveal things was not high on his agenda. Getting others to bend to his will was more like it. Miles' actions came from a place of anger and retribution; mine came from a sense of wanting to put the world in a better order.

"A stretch case," I mused. "Might not be so bad."

"It's an idea. What's your other case?"

"That would be Amanda Hertz, a homeowner up in Mandeville Canyon who was swindled out of some money. She paid a contractor to install air conditioning in her home and he disappeared after taking the deposit."

"Interesting."

"Very much so. The contractor calls himself Billy the Fixer."

"Wow. That's a great name for a political operative."

"True, although Billy is more of a con artist."

"The difference?"

I laughed. "Only in terms of clientele. The guy's full name is Billy Ray Fox. He installs HVAC systems. Air conditioners, heaters, central ventilation systems."

"Sounds legit on the surface."

"Yeah, and apparently he's capable of doing that type of work. But he discovered it's far easier to get the job, take a large deposit from the homeowners, and then disappear."

The waiter came by with our dinner: two steaming plates of blue corn enchiladas stuffed with chicken, alongside piles of black beans and Spanish rice. During the summer, El Cholo served green corn tamales, a wonderful dish made with fresh corn and cheese, roasted in corn husks. By November, the fresh corn season was over and we had to make do with their standard menu, which was pretty good on its own. El Cholo was an L.A. institution. The original restaurant was located not far from USC, and I spent many a happy night there when I was a student. A second El Cholo opened near my home in Santa Monica years later, and I rediscovered how much I liked their Mexican food. The margaritas weren't bad either.

"That contractor sounds like a lovely guy," she said. "Wonder why he went down that route."

I cut open an enchilada to let it cool and scooped up some black beans. "Not sure why anyone goes that way. I guess it's easier than working for a living. Amanda said she was a little skeptical but finally agreed. He seemed to know what he was talking about. And she said he was very convincing."

"So she gave him her money?" Gail asked.

"Yes. A good con artist makes you feel comfortable. Hence, the word con is short for confidence."

"And your client wants her money back."

"And also seeing Billy get what he deserves: to go to jail for a long time. Apparently she has a lot of money and wants to see justice done. She called the State Contractors Board, but they're moving too slow for her taste."

"How much did she lose?"

"A tidy sum of $3,000," I said.

"On the surface, that's a good bit of money. But if she owns a home in Mandeville Canyon, then $3,000 isn't that big of a loss."

"You wouldn't think, would you? Sometimes it's just the principle of the thing. You don't always know what's important to people."

"Sounds like she has a Miles Larson streak in her."

"Maybe," I pondered, taking a bite of enchilada and marveling at how good it was. "Maybe in some ways we all do."

Two

The entrance to the Broadway Precinct was actually around the corner from Broadway, near 76th Street in South Los Angeles. The area used to be referred to as South Central; the name was changed to South L.A. a few years ago in an attempt to disassociate it with the stigma of urban decay and crime. The exterior of the precinct featured an alternating pattern of pink and beige stucco slabs, and the complex filled an entire city block. The area held a courthouse and a police station, and there were some bail bond outlets around the corner. Across the street was a hodgepodge of apartment buildings, churches and retail storefronts. Unless you knew the area, the Broadway Precinct could easily be mistaken for a series of nondescript inner city offices.

It was a bright, sunny morning when I knocked on Juan Saavedra's door. Juan was welcoming the new day with an apple fritter and a *grande* cup of Starbucks. He wore a light blue button-down shirt and a green and blue striped rep tie. Juan's silver hair was cut short, and while he was close to my age, his craggy features made him appear a few years older.

"Now that looks a treat for the taste buds," I started, "although it may shorten your life a bit if you make deep fried dough and heaps of sugar your main morning staple."

"And a good morning to you too, Burnside," he managed, as he chewed slowly and intently on his pastry. "I was hoping to enjoy my breakfast. Then you show up."

"You think I'm here because I need something?"

"That's usually the reason."

"Your ability to size up a situation is *nonpareil* my friend. And you shouldn't take umbrage at that."

"Still with the funny talk."

I shrugged. "For me, it's sometimes easier to use big words than small ones."

"You ought to recognize your audience."

"Hey, you're a bright guy," I protested. "And by the way, congratulations on getting bumped up to lieutenant. Nicely done."

"Thanks," he smiled. "I appreciate that."

I had known Juan Saavedra from my 13 years on the job at the LAPD. He had been a detective at the Purdue Precinct for years, and he was a good one. Juan had just recently earned his promotion and was now in charge of a staff of detectives at the Broadway Precinct, which encompassed a large swath of South L.A. He was also not above helping me out here and there, in exchange for some free tickets to a ball game. And I was sure he knew the USC-UCLA game was coming up in a couple of weeks.

"What are you working on?" he asked, as he took another bite and chewed slowly.

"A couple of cases, actually. The first one involves employee theft at a company called Malco. Ever heard of them?"

"You think I just eat doughnuts all day? Years ago at Purdue we popped a few of their employees for burglary over at Cheviot Hills. They send technicians into the home to install cable. But a few of them developed a second career, putting cash and jewelry in their pockets before leaving. Most of the people they hire are honest, but there's always some that slip through. This still happening?"

I shook my head. "Haven't heard about that one. The owner is concerned about his employees stealing from him though. Seems that some set-top boxes aren't making it past the loading dock. It's an ongoing problem."

"That sounds like a few people might be involved. What does he want you to do?"

"I'll be going in undercover, posing as an employee and trying to unravel what these guys are doing. If they're actually doing anything. The owner seems a tad paranoid."

"I remember the owner. Tough guy, but a real hothead. When we nabbed those employees of his, he wanted a few minutes alone with them. I told him this wasn't the 1940s."

I gave a small laugh. "Miles is over 70 now and hasn't changed much."

"He's not retired yet? Figured he'd let his kids take over the business by now."

"Haven't delved that deeply," I said. "Some people have trouble letting go. He fits the profile."

Juan tossed the last bite of the apple fritter into his mouth and savored it. "Just keep me informed. I don't like seeing people take the law into their own hands. Gets messy."

"Sure."

"What else you up to?"

"I'm also working with a homeowner in Mandeville Canyon. She hired an air conditioning contractor to put in a new HVAC system. He took her deposit and then disappeared."

"That sort of thing happens more often than you think."

"Have you collared many?"

"A few, but the City Attorney considers those things business disputes. He's got bigger fish to fry."

"Explains why my client came to me. Her other option is the State Contractors Board, and they don't have the resources either. Budget cuts. You know."

"Yeah, I know. We're in the same boat. Sounds like this guy's found a niche. How did your client come across him?"

"Greg's List. Apparently he started out legit, so he's got some good client reviews. Managed to leverage that into getting new customers to hire him."

"Got a name?"

"Billy Ray Fox. His business name is Billy the Fixer."

"I'll run his rap sheet. There may be some others who filed complaints. What's your plan here?"

"Basic sting operation. I'll pose as a new client to get him out of the woodwork. Once he makes his offer, I'll nab him."

Lt. Saavedra rolled his eyes. "Gee, and then what are you going to do with him, Mr. Private Police Officer?"

I gave a small chuckle. "That's where you come in my friend. Having a real police detective nearby would help to put another bad guy out of circulation."

"Oh that sounds just dandy. I just love the idea of working for you. So you'll call me when you want me to come and arrest this dirt bag? Is that your grand plan?"

"Well ... I was hoping for a little more enthusiasm here, Juan."

"Keep going."

As they say, everyone's got their price. "I'm sure you're aware that the Bruin game is coming up in a few weeks. A good Trojan fan like you wouldn't want to miss it."

"That does sound about right. Both schools have really good teams this year."

"And the Rose Bowl's on the line. Now that Johnny's head coach, I might be able to arrange for a pair of very good seats with your name on them. Good way to re-bond with your teenager."

"Yeah, he'd like that. Maybe close to the 50-yard line stripe? Two seats sound good. Four would sound better. You know, my wife went to UCLA. Her brother, too."

I nodded. "I'll see what I can do. I forgot you were in a mixed marriage."

Juan smiled. "It's only a problem one day a year."

*

Malco Industries was located not too far from the Broadway Precinct, in a more blighted section of South L.A. that had never seen better days. It was off of Florence Avenue, a neighborhood littered with check cashing stores, nail salons, cigarette retailers, and second-hand clothing shops. Many signs and storefronts looked hand painted. There were no supermarkets, no brand name stores, no parks. A few fast food joints popped up here and there. After the 1992 riots, later downgraded to an "uprising," there was much talk of large chains opening retail outlets in neighborhoods like this. Bringing well known stores in would add convenience and help the local economy with jobs; it was also considered a good way to help re-develop the inner city.

But it never happened. Lots of talk and promises, ending with large companies seeing more risk than reward, more threats than opportunities. So local residents remained forced to drive or take a bus to do most of their shopping, and the neighborhood continued to decay. I spent part of my career nearby, working out of the Broadway Precinct and saw firsthand how the lack of pride in their surroundings affected residents. People became used to the graffiti and decrepit buildings; to them it was just how things were. And some rarely left the neighborhood at all. They never got to see that there was a better world not far away. If someone went just a few miles west on Manchester Boulevard, they would see the expanse of LAX and the blue Pacific ocean in front of them. Gateways to another land.

The Malco building itself was a one story structure, nicely kept up. It looked like a fresh coat of paint had been applied recently. There were a few windows facing the street, but they were covered with iron bars as a security precaution. Around back was a loading dock with a number of white vans parked haphazardly on the lot. The vans did not identify Malco, but rather called out Eagle Cable. I pulled into an open parking space near the main entrance that had "visitor" spray painted in green lettering.

The lobby area was non-descript, with a few metal folding chairs set out for visitors, and clipboards holding job applications sat on the front counter. A gold coffee cup filled with a slew of cheap pens was placed nearby. And a large sign over the front desk warned that anyone carrying a weapon onto the premises was subject to immediate dismissal and prosecution to the fullest extent of the law. I assumed the .38 special I had tucked in the holster under my armpit would be considered an exception to the rule.

"May I help you?" asked a tired looking woman in her 50s, wearing a headset. She had puffy ash blonde hair that did not quite match her dark eyes and olive complexion.

"I'm here to see Miles."

"And your name?"

"Burnside. One word."

She smiled briefly and clicked a button on her phone. "A Mr. Burnside is here to see you, Miles," she said, and then waited a beat. "Oh, all right."

Getting up, she motioned for me to follow her.

"What's your name?" I asked.

"I'm Gladys. Nice to meet you."

"Likewise."

I followed Gladys through a narrow hallway. She waved her badge in front of a square gray panel, we heard a click and the door magically unlocked. Walking into a large open area lined with cubicles, we passed people who were speaking rapidly into phones and moving about the office with a sense of urgency. Gladys led me to the corner office with the name "Miles A. Larson" in gold raised lettering, framed on the door. Inside, Miles was standing in front of a large maple desk and wore an intense expression on his face. Two people were with him, a man and a woman, both middle aged, and both looking equally earnest.

Miles' office was spacious and loaded with USC memorabilia. From posters of famous Rose Bowl scenes to pennants to autographed footballs, the office was a virtual museum of Trojan sports. A full size cardinal colored replica USC helmet, complete with a tinted-glass visor, sat on a shelf next to a row of sports books and framed photos. I half wondered if my own likeness was contained somewhere in this treasure trove of collectibles.

"Come on in, Burnside," Miles said, extending a perfunctory handshake, albeit a strong one. "These are my kids, Peter and Isabelle."

We sat down on a burgundy leather couch, with Miles moving behind the largess of his impressive desk and putting his feet up on it. Both "kids" were roughly my age, in their 40s. Peter was a little taller than his father, about 5' 10" with thinning blond hair and light blue eyes. But he had the same big boned structure and looked like he worked out with weights. Both he and Miles wore white shirts and conservative ties. Isabelle was blonde as well, with brown eyes. She was shapely and attractive, but more in the way your junior high school English teacher might be considered attractive. Not flashy, but not matronly, either.

"So what do you two work at here?" I asked.

"I'm senior vice president of operations," Peter said, in a haughty manner that only a corporate executive could pull off without laughing.

"Chief financial officer," Isabelle offered. "But we're both involved in all aspects here. It's a family business."

"So I see."

"And I believe," Isabelle said with a small smile, "that we were at SC around the same time. I remember your exploits on the football field."

I smiled back at her appreciatively.

"And off the field, too."

Uh-oh. My smile began to dissipate and I wasn't sure I would like where this was going. "How's that?" I managed.

"I was in a sorority. DG. Delta Gamma. You dated a few of my sisters."

I nodded warily. "Long time ago."

"I know," she smiled. "They said you didn't exactly treat them like princesses."

I frowned. Not being sure of how to respond, I said nothing. Sometimes the best response is no response.

"You didn't do anything bad, mind you," she said, her smile still pasted on her face. "But your focus was elsewhere. If I recall correctly, you told one of them there were three things a guy could do in college. Study, play sports and go out with girls. And you told them a guy can only do two of these things well."

"That, uh, sounds like something I might have said."

Being a starting football player at a premier program like USC meant everyone on campus knew who you were. And some people wanted to become friends for reasons not always in a player's best interest. Most often it was innocuous, simply wanting to boast that they knew someone on the team. A few had a professional interest in hooking up players with agents. And then there were the women on campus. It was hard to tell which ones were attracted to a player simply because they liked them. Some were attracted because the players had a certain level of fame -- and might also soon be earning big money if they made it to the pro ranks.

"Oh, don't worry," she said with a wave of her hand. "They got over it. They thought you were headed to a big contract with the NFL. I guess that didn't work out after the injury."

"True. I wound up at the LAPD. Thirteen years on the job."

"Most of my friends didn't marry cops."

"I don't blame them. Most women don't."

Peter smiled. "Izzy had a lot of fun at SC. Mostly driving around campus in her gold Porsche."

"Uh, maybe we don't need to divulge every detail, Peter," she said, with a small cough.

"And I'm not sure I want to hear about it either," Miles declared. "Anyways, we're here to talk about the business. This'll all be theirs one day, and I want to keep it afloat."

"One day? Dad's going to live to be 100," Isabelle smiled.

"And be behind that desk the whole time," added Peter.

"Yeah, yeah," Miles said. "I'm not planning on going anywhere anytime soon. But we need to clean up this crap in the warehouse or this place isn't going to be here when I turn 100. It may not be here when I turn 75."

Peter and Isabelle glanced at each other with nervous expressions.

"Just curious," I broke in. "Doesn't the cable company have their own installers?"

"They do," Peter answered. "But a lot of times they get overwhelmed with work. Their business is up and down. When they're busy, which is typical, they bring us in. We're what's sometimes called a third-party installer. We do the same job, drive vans with the same logos. The customer usually doesn't know the difference. This way the cable company has a lot of flexibility and doesn't have to delay installations too long. If a new customer signs up but doesn't get installed in a few days, the customer often cancels."

I nodded. "Okay. Tell me about the problem you're having."

Peter continued. "So far we've seen a lot of set-top boxes get checked in at the loading dock and then disappear from the inventory. I estimate we've lost over a thousand units. Not to mention the access cards."

"What's your territory?"

"Southern California, Nevada and Arizona. But most of our business is done down here in L.A."

"It's that union guy, Valdez, It's gotta be him," Miles broke in. "He's been itching to stick it to us."

"You know I charge the same fee even if you crack the case," I said, jokingly.

Miles looked at me and started to say something before Peter broke in.

"Dad, we don't know that for certain," he said.

Miles face shifted into an ugly sneer. "Who the hell else could it be? Look it's bad enough the cable company is squeezing us until our eyes bug out. Now I got my own people sneaking out with my product."

"I think that's why we have Mr. Burnside here," Isabelle pointed out.

Indeed it was. And I began to sense I would have multiple bosses. Miles was my client and everyone, including me, answered to him. But this was a family business and family dynamics often get in the way. Plus, there was one other figure who mattered, and she was not here. Understandably, Clara probably had better things to do.

"Okay," I said. "You want me to go undercover to see what I can find out. What does this Valdez guy do other than head up the union?"

"He works for me in operations," Peter said. "Valdez does the routing sheets, meaning he organizes the first assignments for the installers each morning."

"Anyone else you suspect?"

"There are a few of his cronies that may be in on this."

"Does Valdez report to you?" I asked Peter.

"No, he reports to my operations director, Glen Butterworth. Glen says it's only a matter of time before Valdez slips up."

"And how long has this Glen Butterworth worked for you?"

Isabelle spoke up again. "About a year. Don't worry about Glen," she said and then turned to Miles. "Daddy I think it might help if we tell everyone Burnside works for Glen. Maybe call him a consultant."

"Fine," Miles said. "But just so as we're clear, you're really working for me."

"Clear," I said. "But I'll need access to all parts of your building. You never know where things wind up."

Peter shrugged. "I'll arrange for security clearance with Butterworth."

"Security clearance?" I raised my eyebrows.

"We've had some threats." Peter pointed out. "Goes with the territory. Anyone associated with a cable company can be a target. You'll need a badge to enter, and only special badges get you full access throughout the premises."

Miles broke in. "There's a few places you can't go. Some areas just have to be kept private."

"Okay," I said. It was Miles' company and he had the right to have the final say on things. "Anyone else you might suspect here?"

"I'll draw up a list," Peter said. "There's some ex-employees who've left on bad terms."

Miles shrugged. "Most of those punks got canned for stealing from customers. Or sleeping on the job. I don't think they're a part of this. Doing a scam of this order takes some brains."

"So what's type of fee will you be charging for helping us?" Isabelle asked.

Miles smiled. "My girl. Always looking out for the money."

I smiled back. "I charge $800 a day."

Isabelle's eyes grew big. "That's a lot."

I acknowledged her concern with a nod of my head. "Plus expenses," I added.

Both Isabelle and Peter turned to Miles like puppies looking for approval. Miles let out a long breath.

"Eh, look, you're an SC guy, which says to me you're a pro and you know what you're doing. And you come highly recommended from some of the folks at the university. The Provost in particular raved about you. I guess that fee works for me. We need to fix this mess and fix it fast. Izzy, have A.P. draw a check for Burnside for one week's pay." Miles turned back to me. "You have any thoughts as to how best to get going here?"

"Sure," I said, my mind whirring with half baked ideas. "I think the best place for me to start is to get to meet some of the rank-and-file employees. Maybe let me do a ride-along with one of your installers. Someone you've had a problem with. That way I can have an excuse to be nearby watching them."

Peter spoke. "I can arrange a ride-along with someone. Give me a day or two to set it up. I got just the guy."

"Good idea," said Miles. "Show you the ropes. How we do business here. I used to be an installer myself back in the day when cable was first getting going. Figured out I could make more money having people work for me, than me working for someone else."

"Smart," I said. While it goes against my nature to be flattering, it never hurts to compliment the guy paying the bills. Lengthy periods without having any income taught me that lesson.

"So if you're going in as a consultant, what do we tell people you're consulting with us on?" Peter asked, a little puzzled.

I looked directly at Miles. I had been waiting to use this line. "Tell them I'm from the government and I'm here to help."

Miles threw back his head and guffawed. "I love it. You know the score. I just knew we picked the right guy for this job."

As if there were any doubt, I thought. "I'll work very hard for you," I told them. "If there's one thing you can be absolutely certain of, you'll get your money's worth. I promise you that."

Miles leaned back. "As a great football coach might have said," he mused with a smile, "money isn't everything."

I concurred, but sensed there was something more coming. There was.

"It's the only thing," he added with a laugh.

Peter and Isabelle were smiling. I struggled to join them.

Three

The offices for the USC football coaches were now housed in the sprawling McKay Center, newly built and named for one of the Trojan football team's legendary coaches. John McKay was an unlikely candidate to lead USC in 1960, but his unique talents, acerbic wit and the introduction of the I-formation quickly brought Trojan football back to prominence in the 1960s and 1970s. Honoring and cherishing past legends was an important tradition of the Trojan Family. And members of the community insist on using Trojan Family as our designation. Anyone who uses the moniker Trojan Nation is quickly identified as an outsider. We weren't a nation, we were a family. A squabbling family sometimes, a messy and dysfunctional one at others, but family nevertheless.

Like John McKay, and also like John Robinson and Pete Carroll who came later, Johnny Cleary was not the consensus choice to be USC's head coach when the slot opened up late last year. Though he was an undisputed expert on the X's and O's of football plays and schemes, Johnny was not the gregarious, outgoing type. He was quiet, cerebral and not one to mince words. But his knowledge of the game, particularly on defense, brought him considerable respect as a football genius. It was what ultimately landed him the job. That was hardly news to me. I knew Johnny's talents from personal experience; I played alongside him for two years in the USC secondary.

This was my first foray into the McKay Center, and I was surprised that security was tight. Unlike most buildings on campus, its doors were locked, with entree available only to holders of an access card or those allowed in by someone already inside. The security guard saw me peering into the entrance and came over and opened the door.

"Can I help you?"

"I'm here to see Coach Cleary."

"Do you have an appointment?"

"Yes."

The guard motioned me inside and asked me to wait while he confirmed this on the phone. The interior atrium was beautifully appointed, with soft ivory tile covering the floor. A series of imposing TV monitors were mounted on the walls, some tuned to ESPN, some playing a loop of classic Trojan football moments. The vaulted ceiling soared a good 80 feet in the air, providing an open feel to a small space. A gray marble staircase, trimmed in glass and steel, wound its way to the second floor. When I was a player here, everything was located in Heritage Hall, which was a nice place, but these digs had the glitz of an opulent palace.

The guard put down the phone and ushered me into an elevator that featured a likeness of John McKay on the doors. I went up to the second floor and walked down the hallway, past a wall display showing a long list of Trojan players who made it into the NFL. Finally, I found the right office. I knocked softly on Johnny's door before pulling it open. Instead of finding the head coach though, I was met with his assistant, a young man in his 20s who politely asked how he could help me.

"I'm Burnside. I have an appointment with the coach."

"Sure," he answered and looked down at his calendar. "Which media organization do you represent?"

"Just my own."

He peered at me. "You have a website?"

"Not exactly. I'm a friend of Coach Cleary's. He asked me to stop by."

He looked down again. "Burnside, Burnside. Hmmm. What's this is in regards to?"

I sighed. "I'm a walk-on. I'm trying out for free safety."

This time he looked really confused, and fortunately a door opened and Johnny Cleary strolled out. He was wearing gray slacks and a cardinal colored hooded sweatshirt that said USC in gold lettering.

"It's okay, Sean. This guy never provided a straight answer to anyone in his life."

"That's a little unfair," I protested.

"You want to talk unfair, try dealing with the NCAA."

"Ah. Your new job involves more than getting your mug on TV every Saturday. More than getting to wear that cool headset and gesticulate wildly."

"Gesticulate, huh?" he said with a roll of the eyes. "I forgot the need to carry a thesaurus with me when you come around."

"I just like to show off my voluminous vocabulary."

"Right," Johnny said and we shook hands. He apologized again to Sean, and led me into his spacious office, replete with two flat-screen TVs, a desk covered with various recruiting documents and sketches of plays, and a table strewn with Trojan memorabilia.

"This is one sensational building," I remarked.

"It's a step up for sure. We even have an underground practice field."

"Ah yes, for those snowy days we get here in the Southland."

Johnny shrugged. "It makes for a nice recruiting tool."

"Amazing the things money can buy."

"When the team wins, the donations flow in."

"And on that note," I said. "congratulations on a great season so far. Being 9-1 is very impressive."

"Thanks," he said, as he moved a few things off the couch so we could sit down. The early afternoon sun was starting to shine through the plate glass window across the room. "This year has been a pleasant surprise. Some of our freshmen have really stepped up."

"That's the name of the game. Get the top high school recruits."

"Nothing could be more true," he sighed a bit wearily. "Frankly the hardest part of the year for me is after the season. It's a non-stop sprint to get kids to commit here. Once we get past L.O.I. day I can finally take a vacation and rest."

L.O.I. stood for Letter Of Intent, and it was the day that high school seniors signed a legal document stating they would play for a particular university. It was normally the first Wednesday in February and every college football coach in America had that target date etched indelibly in their minds.

"Things were different way back when," I said.

"Oh yeah. For us, the process was much less intense. I

had offers from a lot of schools. And a few were dangling more than playing time in front of me."

"Money?"

"Money, cars, girls, you name it. SC didn't do that, maybe they knew this was my first choice."

I laughed. "SC was my first choice too. Turns out it was my only choice. Both USC and UCLA recruited me at first, but the Bulldog was the only one who actually offered me a scholarship."

Bulldog Martin was our coach back then, a tough, no-nonsense drill sergeant of a coach who spoke in a raspy twang. He was tough on us as players but molded us into men. Interestingly though, as soon as we graduated, his demeanor towards us did an about face. We became elevated in his eyes, and effectively put on a pedestal. We were the special ones who were able to successfully make it through his program. And the Bulldog always treated us like royalty whenever we came back to visit.

Johnny smiled and threw his head back. "I learned a lot from the Bulldog. Even though I played 10 years in the League, he was still the one I looked up to as my mentor. Whenever he'd call me on the phone I'd still practically jump to attention."

"I guess Bulldog didn't have to deal with the things you do now."

"It's different," Johnny acknowledged. "But some things don't change. We're still dealing with boosters and agents who slip cash and things to the players. And the agents have gotten really aggressive in trying to get kids under their wing. There's a lot more money at stake these days."

"And that's why you wanted to see me," I surmised in a lower voice.

Johnny eyed me carefully and nodded. "You were always pretty quick at picking up on things."

"I'm happy to reminisce about the good old days. But you're a busy guy with a team ranked in the Top 5 and a Rose Bowl bid on the line. Spending time efficiently is part of your job."

"Oh yeah. And we have the UCLA game coming up."

"Biggest cross-town rivalry in the country."

" Looks like the winner will probably go to Pasadena."

Pasadena meant playing in the Rose Bowl game on New Year's Day. That was back when there was no national championship game, no playoffs, no computer rankings. The winner of what was once the Pac-10 Conference on the west coast played the winner of the Big-10 Conference in the upper mid-west. Most often that meant USC playing Michigan or Ohio State on a balmy day in January. The rest of the nation watched while it was often bitter cold and snowy outside their homes. The beauty and warmth and serenity of the locale was not lost on these viewers. A lot of southern California transplants pointed to seeing the Rose Bowl game on TV as the seed that propelled them on their journey westward.

"I remember when we used to call the Rose Bowl game the USC Invitational."

"Yeah," Johnny smiled wryly. "But this is now."

"Tell me what's happening."

"Two things I wanted to talk to you about. One is Marcellus Williams. We call him Megawatt. Best wide receiver I've ever seen -- he's practically made of steel. He's 6'5" and goes about 230, has hands the size of catcher's mitts and he's flat out the fastest guy on the field. Never seen anything like him. And he's only a freshman."

"I've seen him. He's impressive."

"Yeah. He's changing our playbook. I'm even thinking of re-installing the square out again. And the bubble screen. With Marcellus in there, the dynamics are different."

"I know you don't like those sideline throws. Dangerous," I recalled. "High risk, high reward."

"With this guy, it's mostly high reward. But yeah, my stomach used to churn every time our O.C. used to call one of those plays. Then I became head coach and yanked them from the playbook. I don't know. If that's what it takes, maybe we install them again. The goal is to get the ball in Marcellus's hands as much as we can."

"Sounds like the kind of problem a coach would love to have."

"On the field he's great. Off the field ... " Johnny's voice trailed off.

"You have concerns."

"I have concerns."

"About boosters and agents getting to him?"

"Yeah. He's money and everyone knows it. There have been some rumors. Mostly agents. The boosters mean well, but they sometimes overstep the boundaries. They donate a lot to the university. The agents are just plain scum."

"Anything you can share?"

"Remember Kyle Otto from back in the day?"

"Sure. He played center. Three year starter."

"Yeah, he's got a business now up in Vegas. Chain of pizza joints, artisan pizza, something like that. Anyway, he told me Marcellus has been there a few times. Livin' large."

An 18-year-old college freshman was not an atypical site in Las Vegas, but one who was enjoying a lavish lifestyle was sure to get attention. And if he were an athlete, it was not the kind of attention any coach wanted.

"Okay," I said, making a mental note. "I'll look into it. Anyone else involved in this?"

"Yeah. The name Larson keeps popping up. I gather you and Miles have been introduced."

There it was. The Provost was the one who put me together with Miles but it was Johnny who passed me to the Provost. Johnny was subtle and knew how to pull strings behind the scenes.

"Yes," I said slowly. "Thanks for the referral. I think."

"You're good at what you do."

"And what is it you want me to help out with here?"

"We need to get out in front of this. If Marcellus has been taking things, it will come back and haunt this program. If he's accepting gifts, we need it to stop. And we need someone to get that message across to both Marcellus and the agents loud and clear."

"And it's tough for you to play the heavy here."

Johnny sighed. "I have to keep the players focused and motivated. I can't be the one who comes down on them too hard. And I have to be on good terms with our big donors. Miles has supposedly been introducing some of the players to agents. But he's been very generous to the university. It's delicate."

"I'm glad you thought of me."

"We can't step on any toes here."

I smiled at Johnny. "I'm Fred Astaire."

Johnny shook his head. "No, you're not. And you have an attitude. But you can do things we can't. And we need your help."

"You got it. But getting through to Marcellus may be trickier. We're from different generations."

"Both of you are USC football players. You've got that in common. You're family in that way. And deep down he's a good kid. But he's still a kid. Look, I'll take him aside and say you'll be in touch so he knows it's coming. That you're a former player, a safety, you might have some ideas for him. I'll tell him it's okay to speak with you."

"Sure."

"And there's something else I wanted to talk with you about," he said.

"There always is."

Johnny smiled. "Oh yeah. This one you'll love."

"Go ahead."

"I'd like you to be honorary captain for the UCLA game."

Few things surprise me in this world. But my jaw dropped at this one. I managed to get a sound out of my mouth before my jaw fell any lower. "Huh?"

"This year we've been bringing back some of the old boys to lead the team out onto the field. We also ask them to address the team before one of the practices. It's good to connect the kids with the tradition. Helps them understand the heritage. That a lot of great players came before them and wore the cardinal and gold with pride. This has been good. A number of former players have come back and done this. The team gets really motivated."

"I'm honored to even be considered," I managed, and thought about it for a moment. "But there are plenty of former players who are a lot better known than me. My NFL career never took off. You know. Torn ACL."

"Yeah, I remember. But you bring something else. You spent all those years with the LAPD. You live a life that has meaning and value. You help people. You live by a code. I want the guys to know there's more out there than just football."

"Fair enough."

"Most of these guys have dreams of playing pro ball. But the reality is only a few players make it. The League is uber-competitive now. Most of these kids are going to have to find their way in life when football stops being part of their dream. I want them to think about some options. And I want them to know there are good and bad ones out there. You know that better than anyone."

I took a deep breath. Johnny was right and I was living proof of that. My NFL career was derailed when I helped USC's campus security chase down someone burglarizing a car. I wound up tearing up my knee in the process, right before the NFL draft. It was a grueling period in my life, but it led me into a new journey and an unexpected career. And I do get to see the best and worst of society. There are some wonderful people in the world, but also some that are absolutely putrid. And we get to choose with whom we associate. Our lives are defined by our decisions. Sometimes early on. Sometimes too early.

"So when do you want me to address the team?'

"We have Arizona this weekend but that's an away game. Next week. Probably Wednesday or Thursday. The Bruin game will be that Saturday. I'm hoping it will be a day game."

"Me too. I've always thought football should be played during the day, not under the lights. Especially the USC-UCLA game. Lot of history there."

"Yeah. But the TV networks decide when we play. We're at their whim."

"It's never perfect when money does the talking."

"I know that for a fact. So are you in?" he smiled.

"I'm in," I said, and smiled back at him. I remembered one of our traditions from a few decades ago. A big metal sign reading "I'm In!" was hung over the locker room doorway. Tradition held that before the game, each player would slap the sign on his way out onto the Coliseum floor.

"Great."

"And I'd be happy to address the players. But you mentioned my attitude earlier. I'm not sure I can check my attitude at the door. It's a package deal. No one vets my talk. If I address them, I do it my way. I have to be myself."

"Your attitude's not a problem," Johnny said with a smile. "In fact, I was hoping you would bring that along with you."

"It's a deal," I said, getting up and shaking Johnny's hand. "I just hope you know what you're in for."

Four

It was pitch black outside when I left my apartment in Santa Monica, not surprising for a November morning at 5:15. The Malco installers began their shifts early with a briefing meeting at 6:00am sharp. Then they jumped into their vans and headed out to customers' homes for their first job of the day. Each installer was assigned three appointments a day, although most could only complete two. The customers who were booked third were apparently out of luck.

A touch of light was beginning to appear in the eastern sky as I pulled into the parking lot at Malco. There were numerous cars already there. As I walked into the assembly room there was a buzz of talk going on, mostly about this weekend's football games. A large box of doughnuts lay open on a table, with most of them gone. I helped myself to a cup of watery black coffee and sat down on a brown metal folding chair.

A few minutes later, Peter Larson walked in flanked by two men. The first was a slim, tanned man in his early 50s, with thinning silver hair that was combed over to try and hide a bald spot. The second was a lean, swarthy man who limped a little as he walked and used a black wooden cane for support. The swarthy man was carrying a stack of papers and struggling a little to move forward. No one stepped up to help him.

"Good morning everyone," Peter said. "We have the day's jobs here. Per our new policy, you're only getting the paperwork for the first one. The moment you're finished and in the van, call Dispatch and we'll give you the second job. If there's any issues, call Glen right away."

The silver haired man spoke and revealed a surprisingly deep baritone voice. "It's important not to waste any time. Like Peter said, call me immediately if there's any problem whatsoever. The people at Eagle are measuring us against their other shops. We have to be more efficient."

Glen Butterworth was nothing like the man I imagined in my mind. While not having an especially disarming physical stature, the timbre of his voice was strong and masculine. It was the type that an actor might have, one that might work well for voice-overs in TV commercials.

"We expect all of you to complete three jobs each day," Glen said."We know some of these jobs are tough, but this is what Eagle Cable is requiring."

"Are they requiring we skip lunch too?" asked a beefy looking installer with a walrus moustache.

"Chase, we've talked about this," Peter broke in, sighing. "You'll need to grab lunch on the go. Eat it in the van as you drive. Everyone's under a lot of pressure from Eagle to meet quotas. And the fourth quarter is our busy season. We just have to deliver for these guys."

The beefy man shook his head and muttered to himself even though everyone in the room could hear. "It just gets worse and worse," he managed.

"But we're being paid by the job, right?" said one of Chase's co-workers who had a wiry frame. "Most of us work

10 or 11 hours a day, but we get paid like we're working for 8 hours. Ain't that right, Valdez?"

"They have a point," said the swarthy man standing next to Peter and Glen, still holding his stack of papers. "This has to be addressed in our next union contract."

"Look, I know there's a lot being asked of you," Peter continued. "But this is becoming a 24-7 business and everyone has to adapt. A lot of people out there don't even have jobs."

"Why is it that the harder we work, the less we seem to make?" shouted another man.

Peter's face grew tense and pointed to the swarthy man. "Mr. Valdez and his union team are in negotiations with the company now. We hope to get this resolved soon."

Some low-level grumbling was audible, but no one else directly addressed the room. Peter continued. "One more thing. I'd like to introduce a new person joining us today. Mr. Burnside, can you rise, please?'

I stood up and looked around the room. About one-half of the installers stared back at me with a remarkable amount of disinterest. The other half didn't even bother to look.

"We're going to have Mr. Burnside do a few ride-alongs with you guys so he gets a feel for the business."

"What's his job here?" Valdez frowned.

"Mr. Burnside is a consultant. He's going to be helping us out in the warehouse. He'll report to Glen."

Feeling like a giraffe in the zoo, I sat back down on my metal folding chair.

"That's it fellas," Peter said. "And remember that you guys have a really important role here, not just in doing the installs and repairs. You're the last line of defense. If a customer is thinking of disconnecting, or backing out of their installation, it's up to you to keep them with Eagle. We can't lose them to Telco or Satellite. Your job is critical."

The next sound was the scraping of chairs and the low murmur of resigned discontent. I waited in line with the installers to get our work assignments from Valdez.

Peter glanced at me. "Burnside. Talk a minute?"

He motioned me to follow him to a corner of the room. "We're putting you with Chase Walker today," he said in a low voice. "He's one of the malcontents I'm concerned about. See what you can find out from him. I'm not sure if he's part of the theft ring, but he's been a problem for a while."

"If he's a problem, why don't you just fire him?"

Peter looked uneasy. "I tried, but Dad stepped in. Chase is a long tenured employee and I guess Dad has a soft spot for him. I don't know why. But I know he's trouble. If I can prove he's stealing, Dad will dump him in an instant. Dad doesn't fool around when it comes to money."

"I'll keep that in mind."

Taking a look around the room, I watched as the installers reviewed their paperwork and began taking boxes and equipment out to their vans. I approached Chase and waited for him to finish eating a sugar encrusted bear claw. A few white particles clung to the edge of his thick moustache.

"That doughnut makes you look like a cop," I remarked.

Chase looked at me. "That's probably the only thing I have in common with cops," he said and stuck out a pudgy hand. I shook it and looked around to see if there was any Purell nearby.

"You riding with me today?"

"Looks like."

"Okay," he said. "Smart of them to have me show you the ropes."

"How's that?"

"I'm one of the few assholes around here who knows what he's doing."

I shrugged and helped him load the equipment. He had a white Econoline van with a number of deep scratches on the side and some small dents around the front end. Before Chase shut the rear doors, he unrolled a large decal that said Eagle Cable in red, white and blue, and showed a tough looking bird watching a flat-screen TV. Securing it onto the side of the van, he gave it a final slap and said let's roll. We backed out of the parking lot, and as we headed up the Harbor Freeway, Chase handed me our assignment.

"What's that address we're headed to?" he asked.

I scanned the job sheet. "Haddington Drive. In West LA," I said and placed the paperwork on the floor.

"Aw crap," he scoffed.

"Why's that?"

"It's in Cheviot Hills."

I frowned. Cheviot Hills was one of the better parts of West Los Angeles, tucked away between Westwood and Culver City, it was a desirable community featuring gently sloping hills and beautiful homes. The neighborhood was not as exclusive as nearby Beverly Hills, but it was considered a very nice place to live. Growing up in Culver City, I remembered going trick-or-treating in Cheviot during Halloween and getting a very warm reception.

"What's wrong with it?"

"Full of snooty people," he sniffed.

"And that's a problem?"

"Wait until you've been doing this job for a while. These people will have you work all day, not give you so much as a drink of water -- much less lunch -- and then call your boss and complain you forgot to remove some bubble wrap before you leave. They're a nightmare."

"Perhaps they just have lofty expectations."

"Maybe. But I'm the one who pays the price for their expectations."

I sat back and didn't respond for a while. We drove through downtown, past USC and the Coliseum, and then changed freeways and headed towards the Westside. The sun had started to rise behind us, and a warm streak of sunshine trickled through the rear windows. As we pulled off the freeway, I leaned over to grab the job sheet off the floor. As I did, I noticed a contraption hooked up under the driver's seat. Mostly concealed from view, but visible nevertheless, was a small pistol. I decided not to bring up my discovery.

"How long have you been working here?" I asked.

Chase smirked. "Too long."

"How did you get into this line of work?"

"Fell into it mostly," he shrugged. "I was in school at Cal State Long Beach. Sophomore year my girlfriend goes and gets herself *pregnito,* so I needed a job to support the kid. Never got my degree. It's tough getting a good job without one. Had a friend who worked for Malco and he recommended me to the Larsons. And the rest, as they say, is history."

"How do you like working for them?"

"Aw, Miles is okay, he seems to like me. I helped him out on something once. His kids are worthless, though. They think they're smart, but all they did was win the sperm lottery. Classic example of being born on third base and thinking they hit a triple."

I laughed. "Is Miles grooming one of them to run the business?"

Chase gave another smirk. "Doubtful. I think Miles plans to be around forever. He's got one other kid who probably could do the job. Works on Wall Street or something like that. Name's Eddie, makes a lot of money. Or so I hear. I met him once, he stopped by the office when he was in town a couple of years ago. Bright guy. Give him credit for making it on his own and not relying on his rich Daddy to give him a job."

We turned onto Haddington Street and pulled up at the address of our first customer. The home was a two story McMansion that took up the bulk of the lot on which it was sitting. The house was painted Cape Cod blue and had a charcoal gray shingle roof that looked like it would require an extremely long ladder to access. As we got out of the van, Chase walked around and surveyed the property.

"Aw, balls," he said when he came back. "This one looks nasty."

We approached the front door and Chase ignored both the doorbell and the large brass knocker. Instead, he balled his hand into a fist and pounded loudly on the door. A young woman holding a small child opened the door about thirty seconds later.

"Yes?"

"We're with the cable company," Chase said brusquely. "Here to assess the property for an install."

"Oh," she said, a bit taken aback. "I thought you were going to hook us up today."

"Well ma'am, first we do an evaluation. Did you previously have the house wired for cable?"

"Um, no, we had satellite. But we just bought the house last year, so I don't know what was here before."

"Mind if we do an inspection?"

"No, of course not. Come in," she said, swinging the door open wide for us. Chase stepped on the welcome mat and made a big deal of sweeping his shoes prominently across the mat to communicate his respect for the cleanliness of the home. I did a much more subtle swipe and followed him inside.

"You know we cancelled our satellite subscription already, so we're hoping to get this handled today."

"We'll see, ma'am, we'll see. Is there an attic we can look at?"

The woman led us up a circular staircase and through a lovely hallway with a beautiful cherrywood floor and colorful paintings on the wall. She pointed up to a small strand of rope dangling from the ceiling that apparently led to the attic.

"You can climb up through there," she said.

Chase paused for a moment. "Hey Burnside, give that a tug will you? My arms don't reach that high."

I pulled down on the rope, which revealed a small folding ladder. We climbed up into the attic and, because of the limited space, got down on our hands and knees and began to crawl through it. There were some pallets and clear plastic boxes stored with various belongings. Chase did a quick circuit of the perimeter and shook his head.

"No cable line from the street," he sniffed. "Just what I figured. Whoever built this figured they'd just slap a dish on the roof and be done with it."

"Is that a problem?" I asked.

Chase gave a caustic laugh. "Only if you want to spend all day here, pissing them off by drilling holes in their house. Then fishing the wire through the walls. We get paid by the job, so there's no benefit to our doing this. I'll tell her the inside wiring is too old."

"Won't Glen be upset?"

"Upset?" he asked, throwing his head back and looking up at the ceiling in disbelief. "He doesn't give a rat's ass about the Cable company. He just cares about getting in and out quick and not wasting time on a long job."

As we crawled back towards the attic opening, Chase stopped and pointed to a small wooden box with what looked like a family crest on it. Opening the clip, he raised the lid to reveal a pile of glistening jewelry that included a diamond necklace, an emerald broche, an assortment of rings and a long strand of pearls.

"Would you look at this," he whispered. "Must be a hundred thousand bucks of ice here. Can you believe what people leave around their homes?"

My stomach tightened as I worried about scenarios Chase might be considering. "What are you going to do?" I asked.

"Me? Nothing. I'm no thief. But there are a few guys at Malco who would have this stuffed in their pockets in no time flat. I'm just amazed at the valuables you find in people's houses."

He closed the lid and re-hooked the latch. We climbed back down into the hallway.

"I'm sorry ma'am. The wiring you have up there is very old and needs to be totally replaced. If we try to use it now it may cause a fire."

The woman shook her head. "How could a cable wire cause a fire?"

"The coating is shredded," Chase declared. "We can re-wire the house for you, but there's an extra charge of $600 for the wire and the labor. Would you like us to begin now?"

"Oh my," she said. "I'll need to talk with my husband. He's traveling today. What are my other options?"

Chase shrugged. "You can always go back to your satellite provider."

"Oh but they were so expensive. We've been paying over $150 a month for TV and that's just too much. Eagle Cable had a special $39 deal. They didn't tell me about this."

"They never do ma'am. You can probably try the other satellite provider, they usually have good deals."

"But won't the wiring issue be the same?"

"Uh, not exactly ma'am," Chase stammered. "Cable wiring is uh, a little different. Cable needs to be able to, uh, carry TV, internet and phone signals. Gotta handle more bits coming through the pipe."

The woman shook her head. "I don't understand. This is so frustrating."

Chase shrugged again and we went downstairs. Walking outside, we climbed quickly into the van and sped off.

"Is cable wiring really different from satellite wiring?" I asked.

"Damned if I know," the beefy man answered, and offered another smirk.

*

Chase called the office and they gave us our next job. This one was over in Westchester, near the airport. Apparently this was a small house that had had their cable disconnected for non-payment. The customer was now in a better financial position and was ready to start up again. Chase and I wired an additional TV in the home for service, and got them up and running in two hours. As we left, he suggested we take an early lunch.

"I'll check with Dispatch in an hour. We're ahead of schedule," he said, as we pulled into an open parking space at an In-N-Out Burger. We walked inside and Chase asked me how many double-doubles I wanted.

"One's probably enough for me," I said, knowing that these double cheeseburgers were plenty filling.

"You got a lot to learn," he said ordering two for himself, in addition to a large order of fries and a shake. I added a bottle of water.

We carried our food outside and sat at a small table on the patio circled by the drive-through lane. A jumbo jet blasted over us, about to touch down on the runway at LAX. The enormous wall of sound stopped all conversation for about 10 seconds. I opened wide and wrapped my mouth around part of the burger before sinking my teeth in and enjoying the first taste of what is truly a fast-food delicacy. Chewing slowly to prolong the pleasure, I made a mental note to try and go to the gym tomorrow. Chase took a big bite out of his burger too, but showed little interest in savoring it. He chomped into a second bite before I had come close to swallowing my first.

"So tell me something," I said after a moment, hoping the burger had started to mellow him, and also hoping he had warmed up enough to be a little candid with me. "You seem to be okay with Miles. But not with his kids. You ever have a problem with them?"

"The kids are so lame," he said as he continued to eat. "They'll agree to anything the cable company wants, even if it makes no sense. They just asked us to add home security installs, as well as cable, phone and internet."

"Is that a bad idea? You're already in the home."

"These clowns can't even monitor their own security. Peter was supposed to have set up a security system at Malco. On account of all the thefts from the warehouse. Didn't stop anything."

"Yeah, about that warehouse theft. Got to be an inside job, right?"

"Probably," he said, looking up at the sky and thinking about it for a moment.

"Think Valdez might be involved?"

Chase scoffed. "Valdez? Guy never stole anything in his life. Peter hates him because he organized a union here. Sal's just trying to keep our wages from being cut."

"Cut?"

"Yeah, cut. Can you believe that? Miles keeps saying the business is having cash problems. You wouldn't guess it from the way that family lives. Unions used to help employees get pay increases. These days they're just trying to keep us at a living wage."

"I'll bet the Larsons don't like even the idea of a union."

"Yeah. Feeling's mutual. Most of the guys hate the Larsons. In fact, if this contract thing doesn't get worked out and they cut our wages, I wouldn't be surprised if Peter wakes up in a ditch one day. Or maybe doesn't wake up at all."

I raised my eyebrows. "Really?"

Chase held up a palm and started to backpedal. "I don't know anything. I'm just talking here. But the installers are really unhappy about things. Our rent, our bills, everything keeps going up and up. And now we're looking at taking a pay cut."

"Doesn't surprise me then that someone may be lifting merchandise. Probably a lot of resentment. So if it's not Valdez, who do you think is behind it?"

Chase shrugged. "Not sure who's involved in LA. But the same thing is happening now in the Vegas warehouse. Worse than here, I've heard. Much worse."

"Really."

"Yeah. Guys can make a lot of dough that way. Working off the grid."

"Meaning?"

"They're reselling the set-top boxes. They tell customers they can offer them a better price than going through us.

They found a hacker who can rework the microchip inside the access cards, so they don't need the cable company to turn them on. In fact, the cable company never even receives any signal, it's all done off the hacker's laptop, so it happens under the radar."

"You know quite a bit."

Chase shrugged. "Installers talk to each other."

"Looks like a few of them have a nice side business."

"I suppose. But I could care less about Eagle Cable. Or about the Larsons' money problems. The way this company is treating employees, if people are walking off with stuff, more power to 'em."

We stopped talking as another jumbo jet roared overhead. I looked around the patio. All of the tables were full, and people were walking idly by holding trays and waiting for others to finish. "Anything else about Miles' kids I should know?"

"Yeah," he said after a moment. "Be careful what you say around that Glen Butterworth guy."

"Why's that?"

Chase swallowed and looked me in the eye. "He's got an in with the family."

"Is he a friend of Miles?"

"No. In fact Miles hates his guts."

"Because?"

"Because," Chase said, tossing the last remnants of a burger into his mouth. "He's banging Miles' daughter. He and Isabelle have had a thing going on for months."

Five

Chase and I finished our second job at a little after 3:30 in the afternoon, and following an hour of intentional dawdling, he called in to Dispatch. As it would be getting dark soon, that would be it for the day. Before returning home I stopped by my office on Olympic Blvd. There were a few calls on my voice mail, mostly from people I owed money to. I'd pay the property manager of my office building on Monday when the check from Malco cleared. But one caller needed some special attention. His name was Marcellus Williams and he was about to board a plane for Tucson to play in tomorrow's USC-Arizona game.

The call came in three hours ago, so using my advanced powers of deduction, I determined he had already landed. I tapped the callback button on my phone and waited about 10 seconds before I heard it begin to ring. Damn Wi-Fi. Another reason to speak with the property manager.

"Yeah," came the voice on the other end of the line.

"Marcellus?"

"That's right."

"IIi, this is Burnside. I just got your message. I was actually planning to reach out to you soon. Figured I'd wait until after tomorrow's game. You beat me to it."

"Yeah, yeah. Give me a second," he said, and for a few minutes I heard nothing but a rustling sound in the background. Finally he came back on the line.

"Sorry, needed a little space. My roommate's gotta learn a few boundaries."

"Understood. You at a hotel?"

"Yeah, yeah. Got dinner in a few minutes and then a team meeting. Listen, we need to talk. Coach told me about you. You're a detective or something, right?"

"Uh-huh. What can I help you with?"

"I got a problem."

"What's it about?"

A muffled sound was heard on the line. "Don't think I can talk 'bout it right now. Maybe we handle it when I get back?"

"Sure. I have an idea why you're calling and I'll help you. And hey, Marcellus, don't worry about this tomorrow. Focus on the game and making plays. This'll get taken care of."

"Appreciate it, man. This stuff is for real."

"Okay. Just remember the football field can be a refuge."

"A what?"

"A refuge. Never mind. Just beat Arizona tomorrow."

We hung up and I tried to remember what I was like at 18. Probably a little like him, trying to navigate my way in a strange new world. But unlike me, Marcellus had been a premier high school athlete, and had been on the radar of every big name college football program in America. He was already a public figure at age 16. And with social media, it was easy for almost anyone to make contact with him. Hopefully I could help him steer through some of the choppier waters. His reaching out to me first was a good sign, but it also signaled that he might already be in a dangerous place.

I headed back to my apartment, and found Gail was waiting for me and had dinner ready. Penne Primavera. She had passed the bar exam but had not started working yet, leaving her with plenty of time to do things like cook. I relished the feeling. We split a bottle of Chianti and spent a relaxing Friday night at home. Just like Ozzie and Harriet, except before the kids came along.

Despite the fact that it was the weekend, the next morning began early, but not of my own doing. My downstairs neighbor, Ms. Linzmeier, had decided to engage in a fitness program. Rising before the crack of dawn, she turned up her stereo and began a full 45 minute aerobics workout. The pulsating sound of a bass guitar pounded through her ceiling and my carpeting. Being a light sleeper meant this was just enough noise to wake me up and keep me up.

Not everyone was a light sleeper, though. I cast a glance over at Gail, who looked as beautiful asleep as she did when she was awake. Hugging a pillow, she continued to doze through the ruckus downstairs, undisturbed and unbothered. Everyone is blessed with different things and Gail was blessed with the ability to sleep through a tornado. I was blessed with being able to sleep next to her.

I got up slowly and made my way into the kitchen to start the coffee maker and begin my day. It was Saturday, which meant most people had the day off and could enjoy things like a walk along the beach, a round of golf, a meal with friends, or reading a good book. Or a day watching a football game. USC was scheduled to play Arizona later in the afternoon, and I made sure to set the DVR to record it. While today was a weekend day for most people, it was a work day for me. My only days off came when I had no paying clients.

In addition to Miles and Clara, I needed to spend some time with Amanda Hertz. She was the woman who wanted air conditioning installed, but instead saw the contractor take her money and disappear. The contractor even removed an existing furnace he promised he would replace, leaving her with no source of heat. In Los Angeles that wasn't the worst thing but it wasn't pleasant either. The police said they couldn't help her. I said I would.

Lt. Juan Saavedra passed me the information on the contractor. Billy Ray Fox was a career criminal who got his start by stealing his own brother's identity. He signed his brother up for a dozen credit cards, which Billy proceeded to use lavishly. After a one year stint in jail, he started his own business, absconding with his employer's heating and air conditioning units, installing them and pocketing the cash. That got him another 18 months in lockup, after which he decided to bypass any semblance of legitimacy. He began to brazenly contract with customers to install HVAC systems, take their deposits and then disappear. There were five complaints filed with the police against Billy over the past two months. An overworked and understaffed LAPD was not going to prioritize this any time soon. Amanda Hertz had other ideas.

"Maybe you can go in and pose as a potential client," she had suggested. "You can have Billy come over and make an estimate." This apparently was going to be my week for dealing with shifty installers. It's funny how some things come in bunches.

I'm not quite sure how Amanda Hertz found me. She had been vague on the details, but that was a small concern. Sometimes an attorney or former client might provide a referral. Or an LAPD officer might remember me from my 13 years on the job. Once in a while leads even came from someone I had previously investigated.

At about 8:00 I heard Gail stirring, so I went in and helped welcome her to the morning. It was a sunny day and a few strands of golden light had begun sifting through the drapes.

"Rise and shine," I whispered.

"Mmm," she responded.

I watched Gail stir, her lovely face and tangled brown tresses beginning to show movement. We had met while I was on a case investigating the murder of an athlete at a local university; Gail had been working for the campus security force at the time. I had fallen in love with her right from the start, and the time we spent apart only seemed to deepen my feelings for her. The thought that she might go back up to the Bay Area for good was a tough pill for me to swallow.

"Are you going to want breakfast this morning?" I asked.

"Don't we all?" she asked absently.

"I'm dining out this morning."

"Really," she murmured softly. "So early."

"I can make you something. But I have a client meeting in a little while. Setting up a sting on Billy the Fixer."

Her pretty gray eyes suddenly began to blink open and she became awake in a hurry. "Detective work," she said, her pouty lips moving to form a smile. "That sounds exciting. Can I come too?"

I thought for a moment and liked the image that sprang to mind. "I don't see why not. You can be my loyal and capable assistant."

Her electric smile grew even brighter. "Or something else," she smiled, and pulled me close to her.

*

Huckleberry is a cute little breakfast nook situated along Wilshire Blvd. in Santa Monica. While not a large space, the high ceilings gave the restaurant an airy feel. They featured expensive scones and expensive lattes. My client was already there, sipping on a cup of green tea. I bought Gail a maple bacon biscuit, and ordered both of us black coffee. The counter person struggled to figure out the cash register, so I made an assumption, placed a ten on the counter and walked away. To my surprise, I had to be called back for an additional dollar and a quarter.

"Hello Amanda," I said, pulling up a chair. "Hope you haven't been waiting long."

"Just a few minutes," she said and looked at Gail.

"This is my partner, Gail Pepper. Gail, Amanda Hertz."

"Pleasure," she said as they shook hands. She didn't ask if Gail was my partner in business or in life, and I didn't bother to offer up anything.

Amanda was a tall, willowy young woman, with stringy blonde hair that curled loosely down her back. Her skin was alabaster white and smooth. She was attractive but in the same way a department store mannequin might be attractive. Amanda wore a lot of makeup, to the point where it appeared as if her face was almost painted on. It was Saturday but she still was wearing a business suit.

"Working today?" I asked.

"Yes. I'm a sales director and it seems there's no such thing as a weekend in my world."

I nodded and didn't bother to ask what she sold. Some things weren't relevant, and in this case I wasn't sure I was even interested in knowing.

"So let's talk about how we deal with Billy the Fixer," I said.

"Let's," she agreed, without changing her facial expression.

"But first," I began, "why don't you tell me a little more about what happened. You said you hired Billy to install an air conditioning system and he made off with your deposit. Maybe you can fill in the details."

"The details are fairly simple," she said coolly. "I recently purchased a home up in Mandeville Canyon and wanted to install central air conditioning. Central heating was already there so the ducts were in place. I requested three bids and Billy's was the lowest. He had a contractor's license number but it turns out it belonged to someone else. I checked him out on Google but I only bothered to read page one of the search results, which had glowing testimonials. Had I read page two, I would have seen the number of people who had been swindled."

"So you hired him."

"Yes. His bid was $10,000 which he said included a big discount. Because he liked me. He seemed knowledgeable and he seemed like a very spiritual guy as well. He kept quoting scripture, said he was very involved with his church. I felt really good about him. He asked for half the money up front. Said he needed it to buy the equipment and pay his workers. I thought I was being a smart businesswoman by negotiating his deposit down to $3,000."

"Go on."

"Yes," she continued. "So the next day he came by just like he said he would. He told me the heating furnace was bad, but he would replace it for free since we had already agreed on a deal. I thought he was being a really decent guy. Oh, I feel like such an idiot now."

"He's a con man," I pointed out. "They're great actors."

Amanda wiped a tear from her eye. "And so he removed the furnace and drove off."

"And that's the last you saw of him?"

"Not exactly. He came by the next day to talk and said there was a small delay in getting parts. We had a lovely conversation. I still felt good about things." Amanda then began to speak haltingly. "He didn't show up a few days later when he said he would. Or ever again. When I finally got a hold of him on the phone, he made up some story about finding asbestos in the furnace. Said we needed to take care of that first before he could risk bringing his installers into the house."

"Did you have any further contact?"

"After constant calling, I got a hold of him about a month later. I think he just answered his phone by mistake. He made up another story about getting injured and being unable to work."

"That must have been very frustrating," Gail observed.

"It was," said Amanda.

"Any other contact?"

"No. His phone number was disconnected the day after that. I never heard from him again. And I never saw my $3,000 again either."

"Okay," I said. "I've done some leg work on this. He's changed his company name from Billy the Fixer to BRF Systems. I'll reach out to him and get him to come make a bid. I'll tell him we need to put AC in my home. That brings us to another issue. Getting access to someone's house so it will look legit."

Amanda looked at me, then at Gail, then back at me. "Will both of you be there?"

"We hadn't discussed that," I shrugged. "Does it matter?"

She hesitated. "I suppose not."

"It might come across as more believable if we presented ourselves as a couple," I said, turning to Gail. "The police will be there, so I don't see much downside. Feel like going undercover with me?"

Gail smiled. "Sure. Nothing like getting a firsthand view of how the criminal mind works."

Amanda wrinkled her brow for a moment. "I'll ask my realtor; she has a number of listings. The houses are empty. You can say the house is in escrow. It's not like Billy's actually going to start any work on it."

"No, once we lure him to a place, the police will step in and nab him. I'll make arrangements with the LAPD to pick him up there."

"The police weren't very helpful when I spoke with them," she glowered. "They said it was a business dispute.

They refused to do anything."

"I spent 13 years with the LAPD and have some contacts who can be more involved," I said, thinking about the tickets to the USC-UCLA game I'd need to get for Juan Saavedra.

She shook her head. "No."

I looked at her carefully. "No what?"

"The police are worthless. I can't trust them. They're just another part of the government. I was humiliated and the police wouldn't help me. They didn't even attempt to make an effort to help. You can make a citizen's arrest. Just get him to come by to make an estimate."

Gail and I looked at each other. "Just what is it that you want?"

Amanda licked her lips. "I want to talk to him. I want to confront him. He has something of mine."

"What does he have?" I asked.

Amanda shook her head. "That's private."

I sat back. "I don't know about this."

Amanda blinked a few times. "Does this mean you won't help me?"

"I'll help you, but you have to let me do it my way."

She looked down at her cup of tea. "So what does he wind up getting? A slap on the wrist? A fine? I won't get anything back, will I?"

I sighed. "Given what we now know, Billy has done this to other people. This is no longer a business dispute, it's a criminal enterprise. I'm sure he'll get jail time."

"How much?"

I looked at Gail. "Any thoughts?"

"In California," Gail said, "it's considered grand theft if

the value of the stolen items exceeds $950. If it's repeated grand theft, he could be looking at 5 to 10 years," she said. "Especially since he has a criminal record already."

Amanda pursed her lips and turned back to me. "All right," she managed. "If the police need to be involved, then they need to be involved. But that's why I'm coming to you. I don't like it when things don't go properly. You think you can make this right?"

"I'll do everything I can. And I'm good at what I do. But there's only so much the law can fix. They can put Billy away and afterwards you can take Billy to civil court to try to recover your deposit. But I'm not going to lie to you. It won't be easy to get your money back, or whatever else he stole from you. Sometimes that just becomes the price you pay for a mistake. But honestly it sounds like a mistake anyone could make. I wouldn't beat yourself up over it."

"All right," she said quietly.

"All right then," I said. "I'll connect with Billy and we'll set up a sting next week. If we can find others who have been swindled, all the better."

She continued looking down at the table.

"And you'll arrange something with your realtor," I continued.

"Yes, she said. "And thank you."

I said thank you in return, just to make sure all matters of politeness were properly demonstrated. Gail and I rose and walked out, leaving Amanda to ponder her thoughts. The morning sunshine was warm and draped us as we walked down a street lined with tall, slender palm trees.

"What do you think?" Gail asked.

"I don't get the feeling she's good with this. Let's see how things play out. She needs to come to grips with it in her mind."

"She's still harboring a lot of anger."

I smiled. "Hell hath no fury."

"That's for a woman scorned, not swindled," Gail reminded me.

"Sometimes there's no difference."

Gail gave me a faux response of shock and playfully punched my arm. "You're something else, you know that?"

"I do. How was your maple bacon biscuit?"

"It was more of a scone. Personally, I think this craze of loading bacon into everything has gone a little too far."

"When we've reached the stage of infusing bacon into milk shakes, you have to believe the apocalypse can't be too far away."

At that point my cell phone buzzed and I excused myself to walk a few steps away, underneath the awning of a shoe repair shop. The number was blocked but I recognized the voice on the other end of the line immediately. It was Juan Saavedra.

"Hey Burnsy. You hear what happened?"

"Probably not," I said.

"There was a shooting over at the Malco offices early this morning. One body found, multiple gunshot wounds. Looks like it was an inside job."

My body tensed. "Someone in the family involved?"

"Oh yeah," he said. "Real involved. Miles Larson is dead."

Six

When I arrived at Malco, the crime scene folks were busy at work. Yellow tape was spread out across the parking lot to keep the locals from wandering in and disturbing the investigation. I parked on the street and started to enter the premises, ducking under the yellow tape.

"Hey you," yelled a stocky man with a crew cut wearing a bright yellow private security windbreaker. "You belong here?"

"Guess I don't look the part anymore," I said. "Imagine that. Thirteen years on the job, all for naught."

"Huh? You got some I.D.?" he demanded.

"I was asked here by Juan Saavedra."

"Who's that?"

"Chief of detectives. Broadway Precinct."

"Uh-huh. Wait here," he sniffed and walked into the building. A few minutes later he emerged with a cup of coffee. It wasn't for me.

"Okay. Go on in. But don't touch anything. There's an investigation going on here."

I refrained from verbalizing the smart aleck remark I was thinking, and then complimented myself on using self-control. Perhaps this might be a stretch project after all.

A bevy of activity was going on inside the building. Both uniformed and plainclothes police officers were huddled about, along with a number of medical examiners. I glanced into Miles' office, where a sheet had been spread out on the floor next to the big maple desk. Juan Saavedra was talking with a pair of detectives, giving them instructions. He looked my way for a moment, held up a finger indicating he wanted me to wait, and spent another minute speaking to his crew before walking over to me.

"Thanks for coming, Burnsy. Didn't mean to interrupt your weekend," he remarked.

"All part of the job," I said.

"I gather you were here the past couple of days."

I nodded.

"Anything you want to tell me?"

"Nothing much to tell. Miles had union trouble, the employees were unhappy about facing a pay cut. There's been some theft of merchandise in different locations, but not a lot to go on yet."

"Basically you're saying you know as much as we do."

"Maybe less. When did this happen?"

"Not sure just yet. Miles gets here at 5:00 am most days, and Saturdays are no exception. Only difference is he was planning to go to the USC game later this afternoon."

I frowned. "They're playing away today. In Tucson."

"Apparently that wasn't an obstacle. We found a pair of game tickets in his pocket. His wife said he had chartered a private jet to fly them out there for the day."

"So someone knew he'd be here."

Juan shrugged. "Maybe yes, maybe no."

"How's that?"

"Miles used his security badge to enter first thing in the morning. No one else did for another hour. But then around

6:00, Miles' badge was used twice more to gain entry. Body was found about an hour later."

"So maybe Miles let whoever it was in. And that person didn't need a badge to swipe to access the building."

"Pretty much sums it up."

"Don't they have security guards here 24 hours?"

"Oh they do," Juan sneered. "Apparently the Elmer Fudd they hired was asleep near the loading dock."

"He admitted it?" I asked, eyes wide.

"Didn't have to. The security cameras back there captured it."

"Let me guess. No cameras were placed in the main offices."

Juan paused for a moment. "That's where it gets a little hazy. The cameras outside the main entrance captured someone entering the building and showed Miles shaking hands with them. But it's too vague to make out who they were. There was a video camera in the lobby that should have captured the person's face, but it's been tampered with. And there's no cameras in the hallway or in Miles' office. At least none we've found."

"Tampered with?"

"Some joker spray painted the lens."

"So where does that leave you?"

"Right now, nowhere. But at least you have an in here with the Larsons. That's why I called. Why don't you go down the hall and talk to DeSanto. He's lead detective on this. I think he's with the family."

"Sure."

"Anything you can find out will help. But anything you

find out needs to come straight back to me or DeSanto. Clear?"

"Crystal clear. As clear as a pristine lake, deep in the heart of the Swiss Alps."

Juan shook his head. "There you go again with the funny talk."

I walked down the hallway and passed a number of closed doors, but a flood of light spilled out at the end of the corridor. I walked down past the paintings of scenic landscapes, interspersed with photos of USC football games. I looked into the open office and saw a group of people that included some familiar faces.

"Hello," I said quietly, as I entered the office. "Pardon me for intruding."

Clara Larson's eyes widened. "Come in, Burnside," she said, her face tight with stoicism. In the room with her were Peter, Isabelle, Glen, and a few other men I did not recognize. One was wearing an LAPD issued gold shield on his belt. Clara turned to him. "Detective, this is the private investigator I was telling you about."

The detective was slender and had a thin moustache. He reached over and shook my hand. "I'm Roberto DeSanto."

"Burnside."

"I understand you know the Larsons."

"Yes," I said turning to the family. "My condolences. I'm very sorry for your loss."

"We appreciate that," said Peter. "This is unbelievable."

"I can only imagine what you're going through," I offered.

Glen Butterworth, tanned and silver haired, moved

towards me. "I'm Glen Butterworth," he declared in his deep baritone voice. "I don't believe we were ever formally introduced."

"I know who you are."

"Right. In addition to being operations director, I head up security here."

Under ordinary circumstances I would have told him that's nothing to boast about, but with the family sitting nearby, discretion was advisable. I said nothing.

"You did a ride-along with Chase yesterday. Did he say anything that might shed some light on what happened today?"

I shrugged. "Nothing you don't already know. Employees are bitter with the prospect of taking a pay cut. They're looking at some union action. No one's happy."

Glen sneered. "Chase is a malcontent. Peter, you should have fired him when you had the chance."

"If we fired every malcontent, we wouldn't have much of a company left," Peter sighed. "Besides, Dad liked him. I don't know why."

"I wouldn't rule Chase out as a suspect," Glen said. "There's something fishy about him."

DeSanto spoke. "We're not ruling anybody out. We'll conduct a thorough investigation here. I understand you've had some theft, which is why Mr. Burnside was hired."

"Yes," Peter said dryly. "The police couldn't crack the case."

DeSanto rolled his eyes and turned to me. "Anything else you can add here?"

"Not much to add. Other than the installers know that

theft is happening up in Vegas, too. Chase told me it's much worse up there."

"Vegas?" Glen repeated. "How would Chase know about that?"

"I'm not a mind reader, bud."

Glen gave me a look and then continued. "The Vegas operation shouldn't have problems. I just promoted one of our guys from here a few months ago to run their warehouse. Adam Barber. He's solid."

"I don't like hearing about this stuff now," Peter said disgustedly. "That's the type of thing you should have been on top of, Glen."

"Sorry, but I wasn't aware of any theft issues up in Vegas," Glen protested.

"I think it's worth looking into," Peter said, turning to me. "I want to put a stop to this stuff right now. You feel like taking a trip up to Sin City, Burnside?"

Sin City. Lost Wages. It felt like Las Vegas had more than its share of nicknames. I had been to Las Vegas a few times and didn't like the place. Vegas was a town where people let their inhibitions down, where anything goes. Simply walking down the Strip allowed you to see a side of humanity that was strikingly unpleasant to me. It was a wall-to-wall mass of people smoking and drinking freely on the street. Everyone from hustlers to pimps to hookers were openly selling their wares. And that was the public side of Vegas.

"Wait a minute," Isabelle broke in. "I don't think we need Burnside poking around into every part of our business. In fact, after what happened to Dad, I don't know that we need him at all anymore."

"We still have a business to run," Peter responded. "And I don't see how the two events are related. I'm sick about what happened to Dad. But Dad always told us, watch the money. I don't think he'd have wanted us to ignore this. That's why I want Burnside to go."

"I can't imagine what he's going to find up there," said Isabelle, shaking her head. "And frankly I think we have bigger fish to fry. With Daddy and all."

"Maybe we let the police handle things," mused Glen. "Or bring in the F.B.I."

"The F.B.I.?!" Peter exclaimed. "Dad used to refer to them as the Federal Bureau of Incompetence. He'd be furious if we did that. Look, we have a damn theft problem here. And it sounds like it's gone way beyond just L.A. This is the way we're going to get to the bottom of things."

"Peter, look, we have things under control," Glen said. "The latest inventory reports from Izzy showed only normal shrinkage there. No different from the Arizona warehouse."

"This is sounding like a fool's errand," added Isabelle.

"Stop it!" a sharp voice declared, quickly silencing the room. Clara Larson had nothing if not presence.

"Now see here!" she continued. "I do not want any more of this bickering. Not today. I don't see a problem letting Burnside continue. In fact I want him to. If Peter wants him to check out the Las Vegas operations, let him check it out. He may be the only eyes and ears we have into what's happening to this company. And I have to wonder if these thefts are related to what happened to Miles today. Maybe it is, maybe it's not. But I want to find out everything and I want to find out now. I want Burnside involved."

The room became eerily quiet. Even the breathing seemed muted. Clara's facial expression, set between that helmet of white hair, held a focused intensity that went beyond anger. She seemed determined and unyielding and defiant. I was surprised when anyone else dared to speak.

"Mom," Isabelle said softly. "I vote we should let the police handle all this."

Clara looked at her for a long moment, and her tone softened, but not her resolve. "This is a corporation, dear. It is not a democracy. We don't vote on things."

"But Mom ..."

"That is my decision," Clara declared with an air of complete finality. "The police need to do what they need to do. But so do we."

An uncomfortable silence hung over the room.

"I don't mind packing a bag," I said, and also thought of Kyle Otto up in Vegas. Going there might help me find out more about Marcellus Williams. Two birds with one stone.

"Good," Clara said. "Find out anything and everything you can. And as soon as you can. I'm not the type that likes sitting around and waiting for things."

I could easily relate. "Me neither."

*

I walked down the hall with Roberto DeSanto. We didn't speak right away and he didn't look very happy. The buzz of activity around Miles' office continued.

"That's quite a family," he remarked.

"Not big fans of the government, are they?"

"Yeah. I just love it when we get that kind of support."

"It happens."

"I hear you used to be on the job."

"Thirteen years."

"And then you left."

"I got fired. Let's call it what it is."

"I heard it was complicated. I also heard you were very good at police work."

"Still am."

DeSanto laughed wryly. "Some habits don't leave you."

A bulky uniformed man approached us. He had close cropped blond hair and a square jaw. "Hey man, it's lunchtime," he said to DeSanto. "Wanna grab a burrito, *señor* ?"

DeSanto shook his head. "I'm good." The officer shrugged and walked off.

"Not into burritos?" I asked.

"No, and I'm not Mexican either. Worked with that guy for five years and he still doesn't know I'm Filipino."

"That's L.A. for you."

"I've had my fill of it. I'm thinking of leaving. Fresh start somewhere else. Wish I could do what you do. Jet off to Vegas on a client's whim? That's the life."

I didn't tell him about the long weeks and even months when no business came through my door, and making rent was a hit-or-miss thing. Or dealing with clients who expected miraculous discoveries overnight. Or police departments that treated private investigators like dirt under their shoes. I sometimes wondered if panning for gold in Alaska might be a more dignified way to earn a living. Running my own detective agency did offer a lot of freedom. But so did homelessness.

I doubled back with Juan and told him of my weekend business trip. After watching him shake his head in a mixture of envy and disgust, I jumped into my Pathfinder and headed back to Santa Monica. On the way, I tapped Gail's phone number and her voice came on the speaker.

"Hey there," I said.

"Hey yourself."

"Want to take a trip?"

"Where to?"

"Vegas, baby."

"Wow. I can't wait to hear how this came about. When do we leave?"

"How soon can you pack?"

A brief pause surfaced. "How soon can you get here?"

It was a little before noon, but being a Saturday, the freeways were wide open. And there is no better time to saunter through LAX than on a Saturday afternoon, when the airport feels spacious and relaxed. After a brief wait at the terminal, we boarded our plane, and the 45-minute flight went by quickly. I had briefly considered bringing my .38 along, but decided I'd probably have no need for it in Vegas, and I didn't really want to waste time checking luggage. If the need arose, I was fully capable of defending myself, and that included using my rapier wit.

The rental agency offered up an SUV when the mid-size car I had reserved was unavailable. By the time we climbed into the 4Runner and headed out of McCarran Airport, it was almost 4:30. The golden sun hung low on the desert horizon as we sped down Paradise Road and turned onto Flamingo.

"So are you going to tell me why we're here?" Gail finally asked, tying her lustrous brown hair back into a pony tail.

"I'm surprised you didn't ask sooner."

"I was waiting for you to volunteer it."

"Would it disappoint you if I said this was a business trip?"

"I wasn't expecting to come back a blushing bride."

I drew in a deep breath. Vegas is known for many things. Wedding chapels were something that hadn't sprung to mind right away.

"We've talked a bit about our long-term plans, but never seriously," I said, thinking out loud.

"Anything you want to talk about now, *compadre*?"

I gulped. "Maybe not just yet."

"All right. Take your time. I've got some decisions of my own to make soon, especially if this job in the U.S. Attorney's office in San Francisco comes through."

"It would be tough to keep our relationship long distance indefinitely."

"I know. I'm also looking into something in L.A. There may be a job in the City Attorney's office."

"Sounds terrific," I smiled. "You've come a long way from working campus security at my cross town rival."

"I was pretty good at that job, you know."

"I remember. You know how to take care of yourself. But you've got the brainpower to do a lot more. I'm really proud of you."

"Thank you honey," she said, leaning over and giving me

a kiss on the cheek. "You should say those sorts of things more often."

Indeed I should. We don't always express our appreciation enough. While my future with Gail was fluid right now, and our relationship needed more thought and discussion, it wasn't something I wanted to focus on today. I was crazy about Gail but also fully dedicated to my work. Bridging that divide would take some juggling. And some pondering. And maybe some compromising.

"Are you hungry," I asked suddenly, moving back into guy mode and changing the subject.

"I can wait. No hurry."

"Okay. I've got a few ideas on some places for dinner. But I want to stop by the Malco warehouse before it closes."

I avoided the bumper-to-bumper traffic inching along on the Strip, breezing past the congestion of the weekend revelers. We headed towards an industrial area on the other side of Interstate 15. This was the other part of Vegas, the work-a-day world that most visitors don't see and don't want to see. Maybe because it reminds them too much of home.

I turned onto Valley View and then onto a small side street that felt like the back yard of some of the magnificent hotels that lined the Strip. But instead of a blaze of colored lights and stunning high rises, we drove past a school for blackjack dealers, as well as lumber yards, recycling centers and a utility sub-station.

The Malco warehouse was situated next to a granite yard, and was surrounded by a chain link fence, complete with barbed wire coating the top of it. The front entrance was darkened, but the gate around back made it look like the facility was still open. I pulled in and drove to the loading dock. A couple of workers looked like they were finishing up, moving a very large metal trash bin out of the building and placing it near the fence. I parked and walked up to them. Gail stayed in the car.

"Hi there."

They both stopped in their tracks and stared at the intruder.

"Can I ask you a question?"

They looked stupidly at one another for an answer. Neither seemed to have one.

"Um, listen," I said. "I'm looking for a guy named Adam Barber. He around?"

One of them finally found his tongue. "No, he left already. He'll be back tomorrow."

"He works Sundays?"

"We're a 24-7 operation."

I looked around. Something felt strange, but clearly I wasn't going to get anywhere with these guys. I thanked them and they resumed pushing the heavy metal trash bin. It was overflowing with cardboard boxes and when they hit a bump, one of the boxes fell off and plummeted to the pavement with a thud, rather than the more hollow sound of an empty container.

Devising a plan, I went back to our 4Runner and we drove off.

Seven

The last vestiges of a gorgeous desert sunset were still visible, with traces of red, purple and gold remaining in the distant sky. We drove through a suburban part of Las Vegas, passing business parks, strip malls and housing communities that looked like they had just been recently developed. There wasn't a lot of traffic though, and I wondered how many people actually lived around here. These housing developments were hastily constructed during the boom years, but the population scattered when the economy began to tank. If potential visitors were struggling to pay their rent back home, a trip to Vegas would be one of the first casualties. And since tourism drove the economic engine of Las Vegas, the absence of tourists was hurting it badly.

"Get what you need?" Gail asked.

"Not exactly," I said. "Something's off about them. We may need to come back later."

Gail smiled. "You certainly know how to show a girl a good time in Vegas. I hope you have more elegant plans for dinner tonight."

"Hmmm. How does artisan pizza sound?"

Gail answered by saying nothing and looking out the window. Message received.

We drove a few more miles before stopping at a local mall. I pulled into a space in front of a well-appointed eatery. The name on the sign said "Michelangelo Pizza." I got out of the car. This time Gail accompanied me, but she did not seem happy about it.

The restaurant was spacious and featured high ceilings. The granite walls and exposed ducts gave it a sophisticated atmosphere. Only a few tables were occupied, but it was not quite dinner hour. The smell of garlic wafted through the air. A heavy set man about my age approached us, wearing a green apron over a white shirt.

"Table for two?" he asked.

"First tell me what an artisan pizza is."

He gave me a funny look. "Okay, it's like this. We make our own dough on site. Hand crafted. We only use fresh, locally sourced ingredients. The pizzas are cooked in a wood burning oven. We get it up to eight hundred degrees. That's the secret."

"Are you licensed?'

"Excuse me?"

"To make pizza."

"You don't need a license," he said, a bit of irritation growing in his voice.

"Are they good?"

"They're very good."

"Looks like you've eaten a few. Maybe more than a few."

A small smile crept across the big man's face as he rubbed the knuckles on his right hand with his left palm. At first I wasn't sure if the grin indicated recognition, or if it was just the evil smile of an old brawler, happy to get back into the ring again with someone who needed to be taught a lesson.

"You've got a big mouth," he said.

"I always did, didn't I?"

He studied my face carefully. "You're starting to look familiar."

I smiled. "Johnny Cleary sends his regards."

The big man shook his head. "Oh man. If it isn't my favorite free safety. I was afraid I was going to have to deck you."

"You still might."

The big man reached out and gave me a bear hug, extra tight. "Good to see you, Burnsy."

"Likewise," I said and turned to Gail. "Gail Pepper, meet Kyle Otto."

Gail smiled that big smile as he turned to greet her.

"Don't tell me this is your wife."

"Girlfriend."

He shook his head. "Run like hell, darling. You'll thank me one day."

Gail kept her smile. "He'd catch me. I don't think I could get away."

"C'mon you two," he said, leading us to a table in the back. The three of us sat down together. He called over a waitress. "Bring these folks anything they'd like."

"Water for me," I said.

"I think I could use some red wine," Gail smiled.

Before we knew it, a bottle of Pinot Noir from the Willamette Valley was being opened and poured. Kyle took a glass for himself and handed another to Gail. She sipped it and complimented him on his good taste.

"Happy to provide," he smiled. "Are you here on a weekend getaway?"

"Work, actually."

"Too bad," he said. "Heard you left the force awhile back. Sorry to hear about that girl. But I'm glad you cleared your name."

I was glad, too. My encounter with Judy Blue Eyes felt like a lifetime ago. In fact, it had been nine years. It was the roughest part of my life, being accused of something I never did. A bogus charge of running a prostitution ring which effectively ended my LAPD career. I still didn't like thinking about it. Fortunately the subject didn't come up much anymore.

"I'm here on some business. Client is a big SC donor. Or was. Long story on that one."

"Spare me. I'd had enough of jock sniffers years ago. First they want to be your pal, then they want a favor. Pretty soon you're practically working for them."

"Part of why I'm here. Tell me about Marcellus Williams."

Kyle pointed to a flat-screen TV behind the bar. The USC-Arizona game was on. "Speak of the devil," he said.

"Who's winning?"

"We are, up 21-0. Megawatt has a touchdown catch, but he's dropped a couple of passes too. Hadn't seen that before. Heck of a player though, and he's only a freshman."

"Dropped passes?" I said, and raised my eyebrows. Maybe whatever was eating at Marcellus was starting to take its toll.

"Yeah," Kyle agreed. "Unusual."

"Heard from Johnny that Marcellus is leading quite a lifestyle up here."

"Feels like, I've actually seen him up here a couple of times this month. The Bellagio, The Wynn, The Palazzo. He gets around."

"What's he doing here?"

"Just hanging out from what I could tell. He's at a table with bottle service and some guys are putting it away pretty good. But near as I could see, he wasn't drinking. Didn't see him dropping any chips at the tables, either."

"Anything Johnny should be concerned about?"

"Bunch of girls around him, probably some pros. That's no surprise in this town. I'm sure they also ate like kings. But one of the men there was an agent. Big no-no. Even if nothing was going on, where there's smoke, there's fire."

"And with SC finishing up with the sanctions, that's the last thing they need."

"Got that right."

"So who's the agent?"

"Guy named Cliff Roper. Has a bunch of NFL guys in his stable. But guys like that always have to recruit. Too easy to lose clients to another agent. These guys are sharks."

"So you think Marcellus is taking gifts?' I asked.

"No way to be certain. My guess is there wouldn't be any telltale fingerprints. I remember back in the day when I was being hustled by agents, everything was handled. Hotel rooms, meals, drinks, private planes. I never spent a dime and my name was never on anything. Things haven't changed much, except for the stakes now. And the Internet. Social media changes the game. Everything's public these days. And the money involved today is staggering. Some of these players are getting eight-figure contracts before they've played a down of pro football."

"I guess you come across this here. Vegas is the place to show a potential client a good time."

"It's the best," Kyle said. "I've got a detective pal at Vegas Metro, he tells me a bunch of players come here. He sees a lot. Some wind up getting into trouble."

"Our guys?"

Kyle shrugged. "A few, but it's the same with almost every school. Before a guy signs with an agent, they want to have some fun. The top players want to get wined and dined and sixty-nined."

The expression on my face made Kyle pause. We both glanced at Gail.

"Um, sorry darling," Kyle said. "My manners aren't always perfect."

Gail smiled a little and shook her head. "It's okay. I like hearing how the boys talk."

"She's applying for a job with the U.S. Attorney's office in San Francisco," I said.

"This may be tame by comparison," Kyle offered.

"Would you mind passing me the name of your contact at Vegas Metro?" I asked. "Wouldn't hurt for me to have a conversation with him at some point."

"Sure," Kyle said and he walked into the back room for a moment. He returned with a business card for me. "He's a detective, name's Chandler. Stand-up guy. Grew up in L.A. actually. Was a big Trojan fan, said he loved watching us when he was a kid."

"Just don't tell me how old he is. I'm starting to feel ancient."

"Nah, he's a few years younger than us. Got connected to him through Coach Bulldog a long time ago. I was having trouble with some local wise guys. Chandler took care of it."

"Wise guys in Vegas. What a surprise."

"Yeah, they were trying to shake me down for protection money. Chandler got them to lay off. He's got some juice."

We talked for a while longer, reminisced over some memorable games, caught up on some old teammates and relived those halcyon years when we thought we owned the world. Gail and I politely declined the offer of a couple of free pizzas. I decided that if I was dragging Gail along on a business trip, the least I owed her was a fancy dinner.

"Where you staying?" Kyle asked as we started to leave.

I stopped. "Uh-oh."

"No hotel reservations?" Kyle exclaimed. "On a Saturday night in Vegas?"

"Uh ... this was a bit of a hastily planned excursion."

Kyle and Gail looked at each other.

"I'll make a call," he said. "You were always better at knocking people down than paving a smooth path."

"You can find us a room on short notice?"

"My friend," he said with an air of finality, "I can do a lot of things in this town."

*

There are indeed some people in this world who can make things happen. Kyle Otto was one of them. With one phone call, he got a room for us at Caesar's Palace, saying he knew I was old school and would feel right at home. As we drove off, I told Gail there was one more stop we needed to make.

"More business, I take it?" she asked.

"Yes."

"I actually like hanging out with you while you work. It's interesting."

"You want to play Robin to my Batman?"

She laughed. "That wasn't quite what I had in mind, but we can figure that out as we go."

"Starting to get a little peckish?"

"Peckish?" she asked, still smiling.

"Hungry."

"Maybe a bit. But we can eat anytime. This is more fun."

"Sounds like that glass of Pinot is working," I commented wryly. "All right. This shouldn't take long."

We drove back to the Malco warehouse, which by now was closed for the day. The scenery wasn't much during daylight hours, but now that nighttime had fallen, the area looked even bleaker. The chain link fence gate was wrapped with a blue steel ribbon and an enormous padlock. I parked near the back entrance and as I got out of the car, I pulled one of the carpeted floor mats with me.

"What are you doing?" Gail asked.

"A little trick to get inside without tearing my clothing to shreds."

I approached the fence and flung the floor mat directly on top of the gate so it landed on the barbed wire. Grabbing the metal fencing, I climbed eight feet in three steps. I swung my right leg over the barbed wire so that I was sitting directly on the floor mat. I moved my grip of the fencing to the other side and swung my left leg over the barbed wiring and dropped easily to the ground.

Once inside the complex, I jogged over to the trash bins. The cardboard boxes were still there, stacked on top of one another. I pulled one down and looked inside. Sure enough, there it was. A brand new set-top receiver with the name Eagle Cable screaming across the front panel, complete with a logo featuring a picture of a nasty looking bird. Blue protective tape was still wrapped around the perimeter of the receiver, indicating it was brand new. I pulled a few more cartons down and they revealed the same thing. Stepping back, I took a photo of the overloaded trash bin with my iPhone and headed back to the fence. I made it back over cleanly, and grabbed the floor mat before landing on the ground. Safe, smooth and efficient.

And then a pair of high beams blasted the area with the brightest of lights, blinding me instantly.

"Keep your hands where I can see them!" a scratchy voice yelled out.

Well I couldn't see a thing, but I lifted my hands to face level, and put one hand in front of my eyes to shield them from the bright light. The advantage of having my hands up also allowed me to strike quickly if an opportunity presented itself. The disadvantage of being in this position was the fact that I had no idea where the other person was, or whether they were armed.

"Would you mind turning your brights down?" I squinted.

"Shut up! I'll do the talkin' here. Get down on your knees."

"No."

"No!? No?! Are you kidding me?! Get down on your knees!"

"I don't know that you have a weapon. Other than some very bright headlights."

"How about I put a bullet through your leg and show you?!"

"That'd be a mistake." I said.

"Oh yeah? Why's that?"

"I'm working for Malco."

"Jumping the fence?! The hell you are!"

"The Larsons sent me here," I said.

A deathly silence permeated the cool night air. The lights suddenly dimmed and I struggled to make out who was in front of me. The parking lights remained on so I could see a little, but I needed a few seconds for the colored glare in my eyes to disappear and allow me to focus. A large figure moved closer to me. He was big and wore a green windbreaker. In his hands was a long object that was probably a rifle, aimed straight ahead. He held it with two hands, but as he moved closer to me, he pointed the muzzle upwards to the sky. He stopped about 10 feet from me and stared at me without speaking.

"So why are *you* here?" I finally asked. "And why the gun?"

"Doing a patrol. I work for the security service," he said, and pointed to his white car which had "Sentry Security Systems" painted in dark green lettering, with the word "Security" in italics. A picture of a large dog marked the side of the car.

"You always point a gun before asking questions?"

"You always scale barbed wire fences?"

I paused. No good answer for that one. "All right then," I said.

"Sheesh," he said. "You mind telling me what you're doing here? Now that we cleared up who I am, maybe you'll tell me something about who you are."

I sighed. "Like I said. The Larsons hired me. I'm a private investigator. Looking into some employee theft here at the warehouse."

"Why didn't you just wait until normal business hours?" the guard asked.

"If we did, the merchandise over there would be gone by morning. This is an inside job. They drop the product in the trash bins so it's exposed. Whoever hauls the trash off is part of the ring."

"Okay," he said. "Let me get this straight. If I wait here tonight ..."

"... Someone is going to come by later, get inside the gate and leave with about 50 set-top boxes. Retail value, maybe $20,000."

The guard shook his head. "I'm calling this in. What's your name?"

"Burnside," I said and handed him my card. "You know, you really shouldn't point a gun at someone unless you're ready to use it."

He put the card in his pocket without looking at it. "You understand why someone hopping over a barbed wire fence at night might look suspicious."

"Yeah. But still."

The guard nodded. "Don't try this stunt again."

I nodded in agreement. "I sure won't, officer."

Unaware that my comment had its base in sarcasm, the guard told me to leave the premises and walked back to his patrol car. I walked over to the 4Runner, hopped in and drove quickly out of the area. I glanced over at Gail. She was looking straight back at me.

"That seemed a little scary," she said.

"Not really. There wasn't any real danger. If he was part of the ring it might have been another story."

"Were you afraid? When you knew he had a gun pointed at you?"

"Too much was going on to be afraid. I had to try and talk my way into getting him to lower the gun or find a way take it away from him."

"I thought of getting out of the car and helping out."

"No," I said, shaking my head emphatically. "Bad move."

"You know I used to work campus security. I have training in this area."

"That could have made things worse. A competent security guard can usually deal with one person okay. Two people and it might have rattled him. And when someone's holding a gun, anything can happen."

The two of us were quiet for a few minutes. The darkened streets on the outskirts of town began to give way to more and more light. When we reached the Strip, the boulevard was lit up so brightly it felt as if it were practically daytime.

We checked in at Caesar's Palace and to our delight, the room was spacious and up high enough to afford a gorgeous view of the Strip. It was dark out by now, but the array of flashing neon lights turned the view into a spectacular wall of color. We briefly debated whether to have dinner at Spago or The Palm or a few other amazing choices. I knew I owed Gail something special for going above and beyond tonight. Lobsters at The Palm were certainly special. Gail decided she wanted to relax a bit, which turned out to be a good thing. The earliest reservation I could get was 10:00 pm. We used the time wisely.

The Palm was located just inside the Forum Shops, which required a long walk through Caesar's plush casino floor. The hostess at the restaurant seated us at a quiet booth near the back, lined with dark wood. Painted caricatures of celebrities were featured on the walls, reminding me of the one time I visited The Palm in L.A. That was a thank you dinner from a wealthy client who wanted to show appreciation for my helping them out in a missing persons case. Gail ordered a very large lobster, I ordered a rib eye steak, we traded tastes and our meal was wonderful. Thank goodness for expense accounts.

Afterward, we wandered around the Forum Shops and then into the casino for a while, observing but not partaking. Gambling was not a hobby of mine. I decided I would rather be lucky at love. It was after midnight by the time we got back to our room, and I wound up getting a great night's sleep on a heavenly bed. My nocturnal slumber was, made all the more restful by the absence of Ms. Linzmeier's early morning aerobics. We woke up after 9:00am, and after a brief debate, decided against a morning dip in the pool. In our haste, I had neglected to bring along swim trunks and eschewing proper decorum was not something Gail wanted to tempt, even in Las Vegas. We were almost ready to go downstairs for coffee when someone banged on the door. Heavily. I glanced through the peep hole before opening.

There is something intimidating about having a uniformed police officer wanting to see you. Having been on the other side of the knock, I've watched what it does to people. It jerks them into full blown alert mode and makes them focus in ways they normally don't need to. Because until the officer speaks, the great unknown exists, a chasm that is wide and fraught with potential peril. In this case, the man in uniform was standing next to a nondescript middle aged man wearing a nondescript jacket and tie.

"Mr. Burnside?' the suited man asked, holding up a gold shield.

"That's me."

"We'd like you to come with us."

"For what purpose?"

"To discuss the shooting death of a one Henry Simon."

"Who's Henry Simon?" I asked.

"Henry Simon works patrol for a private security company called Sentry. Or used to, I should say. We found his body this morning outside the Malco facility. We also found your business card in his pocket."

Eight

The interrogation room was similar to a thousand other interrogation rooms. Brightly lit, starkly furnished and relatively clean. Light green walls and light gray flooring. Old, yet not in need of painting or new linoleum. But it was different for me in one respect. I was usually one of the guys asking the questions.

"Let's go over this again. You just happened to run into the security patrol as you were inspecting the premises," said the crew cut detective, looking at me as he placed one shoe on a chair in front of me and rested his square jaw on his fist. "For your client, this Carson family."

"Larson." I corrected him. "It's the Larson family."

"Yeah, whatever. And you hopped over the fence to do an inspection after dark on a Saturday night."

"Soonest I could get here."

"Oh right. Can't imagine why he'd point his gun at an upstanding citizen who just scaled a barbed-wire fence."

"It was the only way I could access the premises and find out what was going on."

"Yeah, yeah. And then you told him about a theft ring using a garbage truck."

"That's the theory."

The detective rubbed his big face with his big hand. His close cropped blond hair, what little of it there was, stood straight up. He was about my age, mid-40s, with some deep lines already formed in his face. He had tired blue eyes, and he wore a pale yellow short-sleeve shirt with no tie.

"All right. Where'd you go then?"

"Back to the hotel for dinner."

"With your girlfriend. And you were there the rest of the night."

"That's what happened. Any chance I could get to speak with Detective Chandler?"

"Like I told you, he's busy. Maybe we can bring the mayor in to speak with you. How's about that? Or maybe we dig up Steve Wynn for you? Too bad Elton John's not around."

"I'm just politely asking."

"Yeah," he sniffed. "You know we have video of this whole thing, so we'll figure out if you're lying. Better off telling me now. Save you a lot of grief later."

"I'd be surprised if the video told you anything," I said, shaking my head. "The thieves have been spray painting the lenses."

The detective's eyes widened. "You heard about that, huh?"

"The Larsons told me."

"The Larsons. Uh-huh. Did they also tell you they installed a second video camera that gets activated when the first camera gets tampered with?"

"I'm the one who suggested it. But I didn't think they'd install it so quick."

"Yeah, sure. You suggested it. Anyway, we have the video, so give some thought on getting your story straight, hotshot," he said, and departed the room, leaving me alone in the room with nothing but the lackluster walls to look at. I used the time effectively by closing my eyes and emptying my mind of thoughts. A half-hour probably went by, and I managed to enter into twilight sleep mode, not really awake, not really out. Then the door opened and the detective returned.

"Anything else you want to tell me, hotshot?"

"Nothing springs to mind," I said.

"Okay. We went over the video and your story seems to check out."

"That's reassuring. Did you get anything on the shooting?"

"Nope. The camera used a wide-angle lens so we don't have any detail. But whoever pulled the trigger caught the security guard by surprise."

"How's that?"

"He took two in the back of the head. But the camera was too far away to make out much more than that."

"Did you find out who was tampering with the first camera?"

"No, the knucklehead who set it up pointed the lens in the other direction."

I sighed. "Don't tell me you think I had something to do with this."

"No, we called the Larson family and they said they hired you. And we doubled back with the hotel. We figure this thing went down just before midnight and that's right around the time you paid your bill at The Palm. You got expensive tastes."

"You know how big my steak was too?"

"We could find out if we wanted to. Hotels around here are pretty cooperative with us. Didn't take long to pinpoint you at Caesar's did it?"

"No, it sure didn't."

"We need the hotels and the hotels need us. We look the other way when some of the girls make money there, because the hotels give us intel on the people staying with them. You'd be surprised at how many dopes on the lam will use their own names and credit cards when they go to Vegas."

"Crooks aren't known for their brains."

"Right. Okay, you're free to go, hotshot. And take your girlfriend with you. She's been in my face demanding something called *habeas corpus*. Cute broad, but you can have her."

"You know she's a lawyer."

"She, ah, mentioned that about six times."

The detective walked me out to the lobby and pleasantly gestured to the front door. Gail was standing there, arms crossed, looking unhappy.

"Finally," she said in an exasperated voice. "I thought I was going to need a court order to get them to release you."

"This is how cops work. Get used to it if you want to work for the prosecution."

"They're not all like you, that's for sure," she said, slipping her arm through mine.

"I don't fit the mold," I admitted. "Maybe that's why I'm not on the force anymore."

We walked out of the precinct building and stopped in our tracks. When the police want to question you about something, they are more than happy to provide transportation, complete with an armed escort. After they're finished, it's up to you to get back. No car service was provided by Las Vegas' finest.

We called for a taxi, and in the car I checked my phone for messages. One that caught my eye just came in a few minutes ago, and had a 702 area code. Meaning it was a Las Vegas number. I tapped it and held the phone up to my ear, and the next voice I heard was that of Kyle Otto.

"Hey Burnsy, listen, I hope you're still in town. One of my pals told me they just saw Megawatt over at The Cosmopolitan. Thought you might be interested."

Absolutely interested. Turning to Gail, I asked if she'd like to spend some more time in Vegas.

"With all the excitement you've shown me so far? A girl would be foolish to pass up such an opportunity."

"I'm glad you've managed to maintain your spirit of adventure."

The Cosmopolitan was just down the street from Caesar's Palace. It was one of the newer hotels on the Strip, and walking inside was like walking into a palace. From the floor to the ceiling, everything glittered at the Cosmo. A three story chandelier with sparking glass beads hung down like drapes dripping with diamonds. Mosaic tiles with silver insets glimmered from the floors. And the huge, floor-to-ceiling columns of black glass and steel in the lobby were an impressive display of ostentatious art. Even the familiar ding-ding-ding sounds of the slot machines was more muted and upscale. It was a Sunday afternoon, but with no windows and no clocks, it could have been any time of the day or night.

We walked around the casino floor but didn't come across anyone who looked familiar. Moving along to the Sports Book upstairs might provide more luck. And amidst the extra large TV screens showing five different football games, a clump of about a dozen men and women caught my eye. It didn't take a lot to find them. The loud, raucous cheering prompted by one of the games was one clue. The other was the center of attention who happened to be African-American, and was standing more than half a foot taller than any of his companions, and was possibly half a foot wider, too. Beneath a tight black t-shirt and slacks, everything about his physique looked like it had been chiseled from granite.

"Marcellus?" I asked, approaching the group.

He turned and looked me over. "I know you?"

"Name's Burnside. We talked the other day."

Marcellus leaned back for a moment. "Yeah, Burnside," he said, and shook my hand hard. His grip could crush a rock without any effort. I withdrew my hand as quickly as I could.

He looked at Gail. I introduced them and he gave her a much softer -- and longer -- handshake, as he revealed an even brighter smile. I got the distinct feeling that if Gail and I ever lived in the same city, this was a scenario I'd have to get used to. As his eyes took a long walk all over her, I cleared my throat. Marcellus turned back to me.

"You came all the way to Vegas just to meet me?" he asked incredulously.

"Just happened to be in the neighborhood," I smiled wryly. "But I'm a private investigator. I'm good at finding people."

"I guess you are," he said, continuing to smile. The name Megawatt was fitting. When he grinned, his face lit up like a roman candle.

A couple of men approached us. Both were considerably under six feet tall. One was a light-skinned black man, slender and in his late 30s. The other was a chunky, muscular guy closer to Marcellus' age, although nowhere near as buff. The slender one spoke. "Everything okay here, M?"

"It's cool, it's cool. This is another Trojan from L.A. Name's Burnside."

We shook hands, and the slender one perused my face carefully. "I think I've heard that name before," he mused.

"I get that a lot."

"You in town for business or pleasure?"

I pondered the question for a moment. There was something in the man's expression that set off signals in my brain. "A little of both," I finally said.

At that point, Marcellus led me out of the Sports Book. "Probably best if we talk back home," he said in a voice barely above a whisper. "It's crowded here."

I nodded. "This where you usually come?"

"Nah. Usually the Bellagio. But someone knew some ladies over here and so, you know. They're my weakness."

"I can imagine," I said thinking even Superman had his kryptonite. "Are those fellas over there related to that problem you've been having?"

"Yeah. The guys you just spoke with work for this agent. He's really got me messed up."

"Okay. I'll see what I can do to help. Piece of advice.

Don't sign your name to anything, and avoid getting your picture taken. The wrong agent can be a problem, but in your situation, any agent can be a problem."

He nodded warily. "Yeah. But the guy putting the pressure on me is one of his boys. He's not here today."

"What's his name?"

"It's Eddie," he said. "Eddie Larson."

*

Before leaving the Cosmopolitan, Gail and I stopped for lunch at the Overlook Grill which was aptly named, as it overlooked a gorgeous pool. While last night's temperatures had been a little chilly, it had now grown much warmer. Desert weather could be extreme at times, but on this November afternoon it was balmy and pleasant. A few bikini-clad girls soaked up some sun on black lounge chairs that were actually *inside* the pool. Gail ordered the scallops, I had a sandwich, and we sat in the blissful sunshine, gazing out at the leisurely surroundings.

"This is the life," I said, between bites of the most expensive tuna sandwich I had had in a long time.

"A fantasy life maybe," she said.

"Nothing wrong with that for a weekend."

"Not a thing honey," she said. "As long as you can tell what's real and what isn't."

"Mmm," I agreed, as I picked up the other half of my sandwich and dug in.

"So is this Eddie Larson actually Miles' son?" she asked.

"That would be correct."

"What do you make of Miles' son being involved here?"

"Hard to say," I managed. "Why would he be involved with a sports agent if he's working on Wall Street?"

"It's certainly curious."

"May be a coincidence. May not."

"And do you have any more detective work to do before we head home?"

"Just one thing left. I need to go back to the Malco warehouse to see the guy that runs that place. Given that's why we're here," I said, paying the bill. "And given that my client is paying our expenses."

"The dinner from last night, too?" Gail asked with a laugh.

"Why not? I think we earned it. We figured a lot of things out here. We know how these guys are stealing the merchandise. We just don't know who's behind it yet."

We walked back over to Caesars. Our hotel was a block away, but in Vegas that meant a 20 minute walk. After picking up our 4Runner, I drove back across Interstate 15 and into to the industrial part of town.

The front gate of the Malco warehouse was open, so we drove right in. I pulled around by the loading dock first, to examine the back fence. The lock was still on it and no damage was visible. I went over to the trash bins though, and noticed all the cardboard boxes were gone.

Getting back into the SUV, I pulled it around to the front and parked by the entrance. I asked Gail to stay in the vehicle. No sense taking any chances. The main door was unlocked so I strolled into the lobby. As we opened another set of doors, a loud buzzer went off and a rush of activity was set in motion. A couple of people walked out of offices and stood in the doorway. A tall, stocky man with a black goatee approached us. He had a big head and a wide face that contained what appeared to be an angry scowl.

"Can I help you?" he asked, using a tone that did not indicate he wanted to help anyone at all.

"Very tight security system you have in place here," I commented wryly.

"What's your business?"

I briefly thought of telling him I was here to install a satellite dish, but decided to avoid another altercation. If possible, that is.

"The name's Burnside," I said and waited to see some recognition in his eyes. It came.

"Oh yeah," he said, his scowl easing up a little. "Glen said you'd be here. I was expecting you earlier."

"I was, ah, detained."

"Right," he said. "Vegas does that to you. I'm Adam Barber, I run this place."

"Heard you had an incident last night," I said.

"An incident?"

"A guard from your security detail was shot to death. Does that qualify as an incident?" I said, briefly forgetting about the risk of an altercation.

Barber looked me over carefully before responding. "Yes. I didn't know you were aware of that. Last night, this morning. Not sure when it happened. What do you know about this?"

"Only that someone from the security patrol wound up dead."

"Yes," he said. "That was horrible. I don't know what he was doing out of his patrol car. There was nothing going on here last night."

"Nothing at all?" I asked.

"Not that I'm aware of. Everything is fine. In fact, I'm really not sure why Peter wanted you to come up here."

"Word in L.A. is that there's some pilferage going on up here."

"Some what?"

"Theft."

He gave me a confused look and shook his head. "I don't know what they've been telling you in L.A. But we're fine, last I checked. No inventory shrinkage whatsoever. No thefts I'm aware of."

I tried to process this. Something clearly wasn't right. "That's interesting. I've heard from multiple sources that inventory's going out the back door."

"From who?"

"Someone within Malco. Works on the install side."

"Really? I'd like the name of the person who's telling you this. I'd like to follow up on it myself."

"I'd like a lot of things," I said, starting to get a little irritated. The last thing I was going to do was give Chase up because some self-important executive wanted me to.

"Now look," he said. "I don't know what you're talking about. We don't have any problems. You can check the books with the CFO, with Isabelle. No one's stealing anything. I installed some additional video cameras this week when the others were messed with. Believe me, if anyone's stealing, I'd know about it."

"A second set of cameras," I mused. Wherever did he get that idea.

"That's right. I know what I'm doing."

"So then what happened to those set-top boxes last night?" I asked.

He gazed at me and shook his head in confusion.

"A couple of your guys," I continued, "loaded a bunch of new boxes in the trash bins. They're gone now."

"Which guys?"

"They didn't volunteer their names."

He continued to look at me, the scowl returning to his face. "Mister, I don't know what you're talking about. If you have some proof, I'd love to see it. But short of that, I don't know how to help you."

"You're doing a bang-up job of that."

Adam Barber looked around to see who was nearby. "I really don't like your attitude. And you're not helping me here. I think it's time for you to leave," he said with an air of finality.

I shrugged and walked out the door. Climbing back into the 4Runner, I gave Gail a sheepish smile.

"Everything okay."

"I guess. That didn't go very well," I said, as we pulled out of the lot and headed back to Caesar's. I hoped the hotel would grant us a late checkout, even though we hadn't asked for it ahead of time. "This Adam Barber is either completely incompetent or a heck of an actor. He didn't seem to have a clue as to why the Larsons asked me to come up here."

"Strange."

"Yeah. It's also funny how he mentioned I should check

the company's financial reports."

"Hmmm. If something illegal was going on, why would he want to steer you there?"

"That's the conundrum," I said. "Also, this guy Barber had a wide face. That indicates a greater propensity to lie."

"A wide face?" Gail repeated in disbelief and then laughed. "Just how does that matter?"

"A wide face is indicative of someone with an excessive amount of testosterone. It means they have a greater propensity to lie and cheat."

Gail threw her head back and laughed, the dazzling smile never more evident. Then she looked closely at me. Her clear gray eyes sparkled. "I'd say you also have a boatload of testosterone, *señor*. But your face isn't wide."

"True," I admitted.

"And you're positive about this little nugget on human nature?"

I smiled at her, in part to keep her big smile going too. "Let's just say a trial attorney once told me that."

We drove for a few minutes through the near deserted streets as we made our way back to the Strip. It was still warm out, the mid-afternoon sun was bright and directly in front of us. I lowered the visor to block some glare. It was an otherwise calm and lovely afternoon, and things were peaceful. Which is when these things usually happen.

It started off as relatively minor, a motorcycle swerving in front of us. In L.A. this was nothing out of the ordinary; motorcycles often darted in and out of traffic, sometimes carelessly. This was a fact of life in a big city with more vehicles than the roads could handle. But it did not make sense that this would happen on an empty street in an industrial part of Las Vegas. It did not make sense that the motorcycle would then begin to slow down. And as I tried to go around the bike, a large pickup truck moved quickly and purposefully next to us, blocking our path. The driver blew his horn as a signal for me to not get in his way.

I slowed the 4Runner to match the speed of the motorcycle, which eventually came to a full stop down the street. The truck was parallel to us, and came to a halt as well. We waited as a man got out of the truck and the biker hopped off his motorcycle and fiddled with the kickstand. At that moment I sorely regretted not taking my .38 along with me. This was intended to be little more than a fact finding trip. It was turning out to be more involved.

"Get out of the car, asshole," a gruff voice snarled. He grabbed the car door handle to try and expedite the process. "I'm teaching you a lesson."

"Wait a sec," I said, and unlocked the driver's side door manually so that Gail's door would remain locked.

The man jerked open the door and that was his mistake. He who strikes first, often strikes last. With his left hand busy on the door handle, I grabbed his right wrist and twisted it backwards. He let out a yelp and bent over in pain. Jumping out of the vehicle, I balled my right hand into a fist and hit him square between the eyes. I then swung my right arm up high before sending it crashing down into that soft area between the neck and collarbone. As he fell to his knees, I released the grip on his wrist and drew back my left arm to deliver a solid punch to the side of his temple. It was that final blow that sent him tumbling to the ground.

With his partner taking a beating, the biker ran around the front of the car and stopped when the truck driver hit the pavement. He was short and slender and ordinarily would not have given me pause. He kept his helmet on though, robbing me of one of my options. Fortunately I had others.

He started out by attempting a karate kick at my upper torso, which I sidestepped neatly. As his leg flailed past me, I grabbed at it and managed to jerk his calf upward enough to cause him to lose his balance. As he stumbled, I plowed my shoulder into his mid-section. I heard a grunt and literally felt the air go out of him. Grabbing his waist, we tumbled to the ground and I landed on top of him. Placing my right hand against his chin strap, I drove my left fist hard into his ribs. I then repeated this three more times until his body twisted and gyrated in pain. The truck driver was struggling to get to his feet, so I moved quickly towards him, grabbed his face and slammed it into the left fender of the 4Runner. His eyes looked up at me ever so briefly and appeared to do a complete circuit around his sockets, before he fell flat on his face and didn't move again.

I went around in front of the 4Runner and grabbed the bike. Wheeling it out of the way, I dumped it unceremoniously on the sidewalk. It made a loud, smashing sound when it hit the cement, before flipping onto its side. I hopped over the two fallen gentlemen, got into the 4Runner and roared off. We zoomed down the empty streets for a few minutes before turning onto a main thoroughfare. I glanced in my rear view mirror. No one else was following us.

"Sorry about all that," I said finally.

Gail whistled softly. "Not your fault. I don't imagine you

planned on any of that happening."

"Looks like someone wanted to send me a message."

"Indeed."

"Hope they got my message in return."

"I'm sure they will," said Gail and a long silence ensued. After a few minutes Gail spoke again. "You know honey, I've been thinking about something."

"What's that?" I asked warily.

Gail maintained another long silence, and I got the feeling she was choosing her words carefully.

"I think," she finally said, and then added yet another long pause.

"Yes?"

"I think that in the future ... it would be a good idea if you take these kinds of business trips by yourself."

Nine

The flight back home was thankfully uneventful. I drove Gail back to her apartment, both of us needing a little time apart after the weekend's events. She kissed me hard on the lips as we parted, and told me to stay safe and be careful. The look on her face was stern, but also managed to be soft. Like most men, I had a little trouble reading whatever signals were being sent.

The next morning I was up early and was planning to head over to Malco, but a text message made me delay my plans slightly. Marcellus Williams wanted to talk. As soon as possible.

We met downtown, away from campus, at a historic old diner at 9th Street and Figueroa Avenue. The Original Pantry had been an L.A. institution for roughly a century, and it was a place I frequented when I was a USC student. It was open 24 hours, there were no locks on the doors, and urban legend had it that the wait staff there were former inmates from a local prison. While the last part turned out to be untrue, it nevertheless added to the mystique. And while this was still a popular place for blue collar workers to get a hearty breakfast, it was not the type of place you'd expect to find a Marcellus Williams dining. Especially after seeing him in the lap of luxury at the Cosmopolitan in Las Vegas. And I suspect that was exactly the reason he chose this spot for us to meet.

I left a little before 7:00am, so it wound up being just a 20 minute drive from Santa Monica. Had I left at 8:00am, it might have taken me an hour to battle through rush hour traffic. I parked across the street and strolled into The Pantry. Marcellus was at a table in the back, a big ham and cheese omelet, home fries and toast already sitting in front of him.

"Good morning," I said, pulling into the seat across the table and shaking hands. "Looks like you're loading up."

Marcellus shrugged. "I work out a lot," he said. "Need the carbs."

A waiter came by in a starched white shirt and asked what I'd like. There were no menus here so I glanced up at the chalkboard.

"How about fried eggs over medium and sourdough toast. Hold the potatoes," I said.

"Coffee?"

"Absolutely."

Marcellus shook his head. "Big mistake, man."

"How's that."

"The potatoes here are unreal."

"I don't work out as much as you do," I said. Even when I was playing football I doubt I worked out as much as players do today. Everything about Marcellus was freakishly big. He was very tall, very thick, and solid as a freight train. His huge biceps jutted out from a gray t-shirt that advertised a nightclub in Miami.

"You're from Florida?" I said.

"Born and raised," he said. "Probably go back there one day. But L.A. is fine for now."

"How come you chose SC? I'm sure all the Florida schools recruited you."

"They did," he said, and continued eating his omelet. "Florida State wanted me real bad. They were after me for years. But their coaches wanted me to play linebacker. Said I could add 20 pounds and I'd still be fast."

"You didn't want to switch positions?"

"It's like this, man. I could have been great there. I played both defensive end and wide receiver in high school. But I think receiver is where my future is. And I just love lighting up that scoreboard. The SC coaches said I could play anywhere I wanted."

"And you believed them?"

Marcellus smiled a little. Just a little, mind you. "Some coaches say anything to get you to commit. But I talked to the players. They said Coach Cleary is straight with you. If he tells you something, it's truth. Coming from the guys on the team, that meant something."

"I've known Coach for over 20 years. Stand up guy."

"Yeah. That's why I don't want to let him down."

The waiter sat a steaming cup of black coffee down in front of me. For many years The Pantry had given coffee away for free with breakfasts, but like many other things in the world, that tradition had become too expensive to maintain. I waved away the offer of cream and sugar.

"Tell me about what's going on," I said.

"Yeah. It started like this. Some old guys, alumni or something, took me to dinner one night. Told me how they'd like to help me. Think I have the talent to make it big in the NFL."

"No news there."

"Nope. Then one of them asked if I wanted to take a quick trip to Vegas. He said it was okay, I had the right to go wherever I wanted to. And it was on a private jet. A Gulfstream. Try chilling on one of those. Man, they're raw."

"Go on," I said, not liking at all where this was heading.

"I figured, how would anyone know? So I go up there, it's a nice vibe, we meet some ladies, had a good time. The next day we're flying home and this agent, he hands me an envelope with cash in it."

"Uh-oh."

"Yeah. I told him I couldn't take it."

"That's right. It's a serious violation. Same with the trip."

Marcellus shrugged. "They were cool about it. No problem. They flew me up to Vegas a couple more times. Same deal, just a good time. No one knew. But then something happened last week. Night before we left for the Arizona game."

"What's that?"

"They took me to dinner at some place in Hollywood. Said they wanted me to sign with them. Told me they'd be my agent after I finished playing at SC. Said it was all legit, no one would talk until I turn pro in two years. They even said they would get me an apartment in the Marina after this semester. Keep taking me on trips, buy me a nice ride, get a big flat-screen, the whole deal."

"What'd you say?"

"Said I didn't know about all that. It didn't sound right. They were pushing real hard. Wanted an answer right then. But I said I needed some time."

I nodded. The agents stood to make 10 to 15 percent of whatever Marcellus made as a pro athlete, and that translated to millions of dollars. Passing along some spending money, a car, a cool apartment, and taking him on some plane rides were a small investment towards a big payoff.

"And so you went on another trip with them to Vegas yesterday."

Marcellus nodded.

"You thought they were okay."

"Yeah."

"Then you found out different."

Marcellus stopped eating and put his fork down just as my breakfast was placed in front of me. "You know how this shit works?"

"I know how blackmailers operate. They give you things for free and then want a really big favor from you in return. If you don't give it to them, they hold something over your head."

"Yeah. They said they just wanted to chill in Vegas. But that's when things got ugly. They said if I didn't sign with them, they'd let the NCAA know about these trips and my eligibility at SC would be gone."

"What did they have?"

"They showed me some pics they shot in Vegas. It was crazy. They said it was enough to end me, I'd get kicked off the team. I'd be out of football for two years until the NFL could draft me. I'd just be layin' around. They'd see to it I'd be done with football."

"But if you sign with them the pictures wouldn't get out."

"That's right."

I took a good look at Marcellus. His physique conveyed strength and maturity, but he was still a teenager, and teenagers don't always make the smartest decisions. These decisions are usually not harmful and they're part of the growing-up process. Most of us have done some stupid things as kids. But most teenagers are not public figures, they don't get their faces on TV, and they're not on a full scholarship at a private university. And most will not have the slightest chance to make tens of millions of dollars by playing pro football.

"So what did you do?" I asked.

"I bailed."

"You didn't sign."

"No. Everything felt wrong."

"Okay. So how can I help you?"

Marcellus sighed. "This situation is wack, man. I don't want them around. If I was in Miami I could have my boys get rid of them. I just don't know anyone here."

Now I really didn't like where this was going. "I'm not in that line of work," I told him. "I can help you, but I can't do that."

His eyes looked down and it seemed like his whole body sagged for a moment. "What can you do?" he asked.

There are few things in the world more galvanizing than someone who looked like they were in deep trouble and had few options. "I can start by talking to them. You mentioned Eddie Larson, but I've heard rumors the agent is Cliff Roper."

"Eddie works for Roper," Marcellus nodded.

"Okay."

"And you'll help me out of this mess?"

"I'll try."

"Is that good enough?"

"I don't know," I told him. "Let me look into this."

*

The drive down to Malco headquarters only took a few minutes. The swarm of police activity from two days ago was gone, although there was extra security personnel standing watch at the front entrance. I flashed my Malco badge at them and they instructed me to swipe it before I could gain access to the building. My card worked and they stepped aside and let me pass.

The atmosphere inside was subdued. People went about their work quietly and everyone had a stoic expression on their face. I walked down the hall towards the corner office, the one Miles used to occupy. Peter Larson was seated at the big maple desk, poring over some spreadsheets. Sitting facing him were his sister Isabelle and Glen Butterworth.

"Good morning," I said.

The three of them looked up in unison. "Burnside," Peter said. "Come in."

Everyone rose, we shook hands and Peter went and closed the door. Motioning us to sit, we all moved over to the burgundy couch.

"I'm surprised you're working today," I said. "All things considered."

Isabelle sighed. "The business needs attention. Someone

has to run it. But our brother is in town. He's with our mom."

"I'd like to meet him," I said.

Butterworth frowned. "Why's that?" he asked in the deep voice that was starting to get under my skin.

"His name has come up. Ancillary investigation. Don't think it has anything to do with Malco."

"Uh-huh," Peter said blankly and then changed the subject. "I heard there was a murder in Vegas. Security guard. Awful thing," Peter said.

"Awful," I repeated.

"Tell me what you found out there."

"You have thieves working in your Vegas operation," I said.

"You're sure?"

"I'm sure."

"How do you know this?" Isabelle asked, eyes wide.

I pulled out my phone and showed them the pictures of the brand new set-top boxes that had been discarded in the trash.

"Someone's throwing away product?" Peter asked.

"No. They're dumping brand new receivers in the trash. Looks like empty boxes from a distance. Then late at night someone comes by, maybe in a garbage truck, and takes the receivers away."

"Good lord," Isabelle said. "That's outrageous. Did you see who was doing this?"

"Yeah. Couple of guys working on the loading dock. Didn't see any badges on them. Hard to tell if they were employees or not."

"And I'll bet they're the ones who spray painted the

security cameras," Butterworth mused.

"Yeah, funny thing about that. Barber said he installed a second set of video cameras that got activated when the first cameras were tampered with."

"I know," Peter said. "Dad ordered them installed last week."

"Problem is the cameras aren't facing the loading dock," I said. "They're facing the fence. And they didn't have a zoom on them, so all we got are some wide shots that don't show much. Whoever killed the security guard was too far away to be identified."

"And these guys got onto the property in the middle of the night."

"Yeah. There was no damage to the fence and the lock hadn't been broken. So I'm thinking whoever stole the merchandise most likely had a key."

"Maybe it was the garbage company," Isabelle suggested.

"They don't usually work in the middle of the night on a Saturday. And even if it was, someone on the inside was moving product into the trash bins."

The three of them sat back and looked askance. Peter and Isabelle appeared lost, as if waiting for someone like Miles to step in and give them guidance.

"I would bet the same tactic is being used here," I continued.

Peter looked at Butterworth. "You need to make sure the new cameras are pointed directly at the trash bins. I want to know who's wheeling this stuff out."

"Sure," Glen said, continuing to frown."I don't get how that could have happened."

I looked around at the nicely appointed office. "And one other thing. My interaction with Adam Barber left something to be desired."

"How so?" Peter asked.

"He said there was no merchandise being stolen and the inventory reflects that. He told me to go look at the books and I'd see."

Isabelle glared at me. "We're not showing our financial reports to an outsider," she said in a miffed voice. "You're just here to investigate theft of merchandise."

"And that's what I'm doing," I responded evenly. "Of course I may have to bill you for combat pay."

"What are you talking about? We're paying you an awful lot."

"And I'm earning it. After I left the Vegas warehouse, a couple of thugs tried to rough me up. They picked on the wrong guy."

"Who were they?" Peter asked.

"They weren't kind enough to tell me their names. They were driving a white pickup and a motorcycle. They ran me off the road and started something. I finished it."

"You don't think they're with our company, do you?"

"I have no idea, Peter," I shrugged. "Maybe they're just goons Barber hired on the side. I don't mind cleaning their clocks, but it strikes me that not everyone in management here is working towards the same goal."

"And you think Barber's part of all this?" Peter asked.

"He sure didn't seem happy I was looking into things. And he didn't respond to the tip on how the product is going out through the trash bins."

"Sometimes in companies," Isabelle said, "People get into self-preservation mode. Maybe he felt you were intruding in his area."

"I was."

"I'll talk to him," Peter said. "We have enough issues to deal with. We don't need any more political in-fighting."

"More political infighting?" I asked.

Peter and Isabelle glanced at one another haltingly. "It's a family matter, Burnside," Peter said.

"Okay. I don't need to look into every nook and cranny of your business. And I certainly wasn't implying you need to show me your books. But all of this seems interwoven. In a family business, the family and the business get hard to separate."

"Look we appreciate what you've found out," Isabelle said. "And I don't mean to sound ungrateful, but I'm not sure how you can help us going forward. We'll pay you for your time, but I think we have a good handle on things now."

"Thank you for the compliments," I said. "But you didn't hire me. Your parents did. And until your mother tells me otherwise, I'm still working this case. I owe it to her and I owe it to your father."

Peter tilted his head. "Just what else do you think you can come up with? Who killed Dad?"

"I don't know. Ultimately that's the job of the police. But something related to the business resulted in your father getting shot. So maybe I can help here."

At that point, the door opened and in walked a short, well-built man with long blond hair. He moved with a strut and had a cocky expression on his face.

"Well excuse me," the little man said, using a big voice. "I do hope I'm not interrupting an important board meeting. One I wasn't invited to."

Peter looked at him oddly. "We weren't expecting you here this morning," he said. "I figured we'd see you later today at the house."

"I thought I'd stop by and see how things were going," he mused and looked at me pointedly. "I don't think I know you."

"Your loss," I replied.

The man smirked. "What's your name?"

"Burnside. What's yours?"

"Eddie Larson," he said, and reached out to shake my hand. "I've heard your name tossed around. Figured you might be here."

Ten

As an only child, I never got to experience the relationship between siblings. My psychology classes taught me while they share the same parents, grow up in the same household, and have physical traits in common, they could often have remarkably different personalities. Depending upon the tone the parents set in the household, their relationships could be very close or very strained.

My reading on the subject taught me that older siblings are sometimes favored, leaving younger ones pining for parental attention. This pining does not always go away when they reach adulthood. Without a much stronger background in psychology, and lacking a deep interaction with the Larson clan, I could only make superficial judgments. But from what I saw, these siblings had very complicated relationships, with both each other and with their father. And when a lot of money is thrown into the mix, the situation could only get more complex.

The molecules of the office changed immediately when Eddie Larson walked in. Peter and Isabelle seemed very uncomfortable, and quickly excused themselves to go back to work. I got the distinct feeling they were happy to distance themselves from their younger brother. Eddie suggested we take a stroll around the office.

"It's been a few years since I walked through this place," Eddie mused.

"I hear you work on Wall Street."

"Something like that."

"That's an interesting answer. Either you do or you don't."

"I work for some very influential people. High up in the investment banking world. I'm something of a consultant. A problem solver. A fixer."

"Sounds a little like what I do. Except I'm better at taking things apart than fixing them."

"Ha," he said absently, looking down the hall. "Just what do you do?"

"Private investigator."

He didn't answer right away, taking his time thinking about it. "Mom hire you?"

"No, it was your Dad."

Eddie looked at me. "Why?"

"He believed there was employee theft going on here."

"Find anything?"

"Yes. It's happening in Vegas. Most likely here too, but there's no direct proof yet."

"Who's doing it? My money's on the union guy."

"That's what your father thought. No indication that's the case."

"Therefore you're still poking around," he mused.

"Still am."

Eddie laughed. "You sound like a consultant. Just like me. You go in and work on one problem and you find a few more. Rack up those billable hours."

I shook my head. "That's not what I do."

Eddie waved me off. "Relax. I get it," he said.

I stopped for a moment to get his full attention. "So how did you come to know Marcellus Williams?"

He studied my face and didn't answer right away. Eddie had the same clear blue eyes as his brother and father. Their features had similarities. But while Miles and Peter were intense and earnest, Eddie was light and breezy. I got the feeling not much worried him.

"How do *you* know him?" he asked, invoking the old saw of answering a question with a question.

"I used to play football with Johnny Cleary. Back in the day."

"Oh, you're an SC guy? That explains it."

"Explains what?"

"Why Dad hired you. Crazy about the Trojans. He bled cardinal and gold. Got Peter and Izzy into it, too. I'm the black sheep. I never got into all that 'Fight On' stuff."

I understood. Years ago I recall seeing someone wearing a t-shirt that said "It's a USC Thing" on the front of the shirt, and "You Wouldn't Understand" printed on the back. It seemed to capture the wide chasm between Trojan fans and non-fans.

"USC's a place that's about tradition and legacy. They focus on keeping the heritage going," I told him, "but it's not that different from a lot of other schools. We've just won more football games."

"Yeah, Dad was into that. Big time. Uh, how much do you know Marcellus and his situation?"

"I know some things. He's worried about keeping his eligibility. Some agents are pressing him to sign with them."

Eddie laughed. "Imagine that. Agents behaving badly."

"So what's your involvement with Marcellus?"

"I'm just the front guy," he said. "I'm working for some people who are trying to sign him. I get a commission if it happens."

"And if it doesn't?"

"I have other ways to make a living," Eddie shrugged. "I got involved here because of some connections."

"Marcellus would like you guys to back off."

Eddie folded his arms onto his chest. "That's not how agents work. Not in their DNA. Like salmon. They only swim upstream."

"Is blackmail in their DNA?" I asked, watching him carefully.

He let out a chuckle. "I'd be a little careful about throwing that term around."

I felt a little anger building. "And I'd be a little careful about moving forward with releasing anything about Marcellus. The only ones you'll hurt are the kid himself and people who follow the football program and care about the university."

Eddie sneered. "Like I give a damn about them. Pack of old farts. I get tired of the rah-rah junk. These players today are just biding their time until they're eligible for the NFL. They have to be three years out of high school before they can play pro football. What a racket. In the NBA they only have to put in one year of college. In baseball they can jump straight to the big leagues, right out of high school."

"This is football. They have to wait their turn. So do the agents."

"Hey, it's all about making that coin. The sooner they

start getting paid for what they do, the happier they are. This college sports stuff is all about the money. Everything's about money."

I thought back to all the time I spent as an athlete in college. Working in the weight room, running miles each day, doing drills. The NFL had been a dream of mine too, but I knew it could be fleeting. The injury to my knee ended my career in pro football before it even started.

But as they say, when one door closes, another one opens, and that door led me into a career in law enforcement. It was certainly not as lucrative, but it gave me a certain satisfaction that sports did not. And pro football careers have a small shelf life. The average tenure in the NFL is very limited, and once you're done, you're done. Some players go into broadcasting or coaching or scouting or working in the front office. But most drift into other things. And while the money can be big, for many athletes it's gone in a very short time.

"I wouldn't call it a racket," I said, trying to choose my words carefully and not blow up. "But to an outsider, I can see why you might be cynical about it."

"It's all about money," he continued. "Everything is. Colleges, sports, this place here. I'll bet Dad was killed over money."

"Is that what you think?" I asked in a low voice.

"I don't know," he said. "Maybe. Probably. Who knows. I have a feeling the truth may never come out."

I didn't respond, partly because I had a nagging feeling Eddie might be right about that.

"Don't worry so much about Marcellus," he continued.

"These things take care of themselves. Everything will be okay with the kid. The agent doesn't want to hurt him. Marcellus' success is his success. You'll see."

I didn't say anything, and at this point we were near the loading dock. Eddie said he had some things to discuss with his brother and sister. He gave me his mother's address in Manhattan Beach and told me I should stop by and visit her. She was in mourning but she seemed to perk up when SC people dropped by.

"We see things differently, but I appreciate your trying to help my family," he said, as he slapped me on the shoulder and walked away.

*

I watched Eddie Larson walk down the hall as I tried to sort out our conversation. But before I could get very far, I heard my name being called.

"*Señor* Burnside?"

I turned and saw a slender Latino man moving awkwardly towards me. He used a black cane to steady himself, and hobbled a little as he walked. I recognized him as Sal Valdez, the union shop steward.

"Have you a moment?" he asked.

"Sure," I said and followed him to his office. Unlike the richly upholstered, plush surroundings of Miles' office, Valdez' space was small and spartan. He had a gray metal desk that held some stackable letter trays, a round pencil cup with a dozen pens of varying sizes standing in it, and lots of papers spread here and there. Half a cup of cream laden coffee sat nearby. Valdez closed the door behind us.

"Please sit down," he said.

"You have a third leg," I observed.

"What?"

"You're using a cane to help you walk."

"Oh yes. I had hip replacement surgery a few weeks ago."

"That's a pretty quick recovery period."

"It still hurts. But there have been great advancements in the surgical field. This is now considered a routine procedure. The cane helps, it's incredibly sturdy. And I'm walking over a mile a day now, so I am improving."

I pulled a hard folding chair lined with scratched paint towards me and eased down into it. "What's on your mind?" I asked.

"Have you found out anything about Miles' death? Who was involved? Anything at all?"

I shook my head. "No. That's the job of the police. Why?"

"It's vital that the killer be apprehended. Quickly."

"I would agree. What's your concern?"

He drew in a deep breath. "The police have labeled me as a person of interest in the murder."

"Tell me more. How did they come up with that in their investigation?"

"They have no proof, they've backed into it. I forgot my badge on Saturday morning. Miles let me in. He was near the entrance. It seemed like he was waiting for someone."

"Meaning?" I asked.

"He seemed surprised to see me. And he kept looking past me to see if anyone else was coming."

"You normally work Saturdays?"

"Nights, weekends. I work very hard. I spend long hours here. In addition to my regular duties, I've taken on being the union rep."

"So Miles let you into the building."

"Yes. I went into my office and began working. That was about 6:00am. I have to be here early. Then maybe an hour later I heard screaming down the hall. I went down to see what was happening and there was the body."

"Who found him?"

"One of the clerical people. She went in to get a signature or something. Apparently he had been dead for close to an hour."

"Around the time you arrived at the office."

"Yes."

"So how did the police make the jump to start considering you?"

Valdez wiped his face and looked down at the floor. "My entry into the building was recorded. They say Miles let in two people around that time. I was one of them. I acknowledged that. They haven't found the other person."

"And the video cameras weren't focused on anyone's face."

"No. And the combination of the union dispute, along with my early arrival has the police trying to link me to the murder."

"Let me ask you a question. Do you happen to own a gun?"

Valdez took another deep breath, "I do. I have several, although I was reluctant to tell the police initially. They have them now. The police did a full search of my home yesterday, but obviously they didn't come up with anything concrete, because I didn't do this. My guns haven't been fired in over a month, the last time I went to the target range. And Miles was shot with a different type of gun, but the police are still looking at me as a suspect. I have no idea why."

It was my turn to take a deep breath. There was no good way yet to confirm or deny whether Valdez was being honest. But the fact that he sought my help was one small indication that he might be telling the truth. People who are guilty often obfuscate the facts to try to create an alibi they can hide behind. Some often show no fear whatsoever and practically dare law enforcement to find something. Valdez didn't strike me as displaying either of these indicators.

"Who is the investigating officer?" I asked.

"Roberto DeSanto. I thought he might be Latino also, so he might give me the benefit of the doubt."

"Don't count on it," I warned. "Even if he shares your ethnic background, cops have no mercy on their own. Their reference group is other cops." I didn't bother to inform him DeSanto was actually Filipino.

"Then how do I prove my innocence?" he implored.

"Cooperate. Don't hide anything. If they suspect you're not being up front with them, they'll look for anything and everything to tie you to this. Good cops don't manufacture evidence, but there's nothing to say they won't arrest you on what they've got, and then let the City Attorney sort it out. Stranger things have happened."

Valdez kept looking down at the floor. The linoleum was pretty battered but something else was eating at him.

"Anything more you want to share?" I asked.

"With Miles, um, gone, there's rumors of layoffs. There are financial problems with this company. They seem to go way beyond the thievery."

"How do you know this?"

"It's an open secret. People talk. The cable company has made so many demands, they threaten to stop doing business with us unless we comply. They are always setting greater requirements for us and then cutting our pay if we don't fully deliver. I felt for Miles. He had to make some tough decisions."

I sat back. It was hardly a stretch to think the thefts, the financial issues and Miles' death were somehow connected. "Go on," I said.

"Even with Miles still here, this was being rumored. Plus, Miles had a love-hate relationship with the employees. He appreciated the work we did, but felt all of the money belonged in his pockets. With Peter and Isabelle it's not love-hate. There's no love there at all. They have dollar bills in their hearts."

I shrugged. "Sounds like a lot of business people I've met over the years. Remember that we're all here for a reason. The purpose of a business is to make money. How the money gets divvied up is where things sometimes get dicey."

Valdez nodded quickly. "You seem very wise."

"I'll let you know if I come up with anything that can help you," I said, and then I thought of something. "Sal, if you're aware of any financial improprieties here at Malco, that's something which could assist both of us. It would be really helpful if you could provide some documentation. You might be the only one who's close enough to get to this info."

Sal sighed. "I'm aware of quite a bit. Getting documentation is another story. Let me see what I can do."

We shook hands and I walked out the door and down the hall. I had no idea who killed Miles, who was stealing from the company, or if anybody in the business world ever bothered to tell anyone the whole truth. I sometimes felt I had a much easier assignment in my career. Dealing with hardened criminals.

*

It was a short drive from the Malco offices to the Broadway Precinct. It was mid-morning and a hazy, milky white sky was stretched over South L.A. The temperature was warm, and filtered sunlight struggled to crack through the layers of smog. By mid-afternoon this area would likely be treated to a blue sky and clear sunshine. But it often required a few hours for the sun to burn its way through the marine layer that often engulfed the region.

Juan Saavedra was reviewing some papers and was leaning back in his chair. A pair of rimless glasses sat at the tip of his nose. I knocked as I entered, and sat down on a vinyl covered blue chair facing the desk. Juan looked up.

"You should consider bifocals," I said.

"Thanks for the tip," he said. "Just make yourself at home there, Burnsy."

"I try to be comfortable wherever life takes me."

"Uh-huh. Nice attitude you got there. Let me know when you want to join the rest of us. Have a good time up in Vegas? Hope the dice tables were hot."

"I'm not big on gambling. I prefer sure things."

"You should play the stock market, Burnsy."

"Isn't that a form of gambling?"

"Not the way Wall Street runs things."

"Cynical this morning, aren't we?" I commented.

"I've had better days. How's the Malco investigation going?"

"I was going to ask you the same thing. I heard you have Sal Valdez as a person of interest."

Juan shrugged. "We don't have a lot. We know he was let into the building by the victim. Doesn't mean anything, there were a few others already there, and Miles let someone else in also. But Valdez has some holes in his story. First he told us he didn't own a gun but turns out he's got three of them in his house."

"And none of them are a match with the murder weapon."

"That's right," he sighed. "Valdez and Miles had their differences, but it still doesn't add up to murder. At least not yet. We also learned a few of the installers have criminal records. I think you did a ride-along with one of them."

"Chase?" I asked.

"Yeah, little tough guy with the oversized moustache? Damn, I can't figure out how he eats with that thing."

"What was his rap sheet like?"

"Mostly this and that. A DUI, disturbing the peace, a few assault and battery charges. Oh yeah, carrying a concealed weapon. A couple of those charges stuck, he's on probation. One more and he gets jail time for sure."

If it's murder, he'll go away for good, I thought grimly.

"Is he a suspect?" I asked.

"Don't know. He had a few dealings with Miles, but from what I can gather they worked together okay. Still, we're keeping an eye on him. Anything you care to share?"

I shook my head. "Nothing unusual. Chase said Miles liked him. Helped Miles out in some way. That might be worth following up on. I think Chase may know something. But what I know about Chase is pretty vague."

"Yeah, everything here is pretty vague. We're about as close to solving this one as Vegas Metro is to solving that security guard murder."

"You heard about that one."

"You forget that us cops talk to each other? Two murders in two days, each one related to the same company, Malco?"

"I'm still trying to piece all this together myself," I said. "There's definitely employee theft going on. Maybe Miles found out who it was and confronted them. But that doesn't explain Vegas."

"Nope. The pieces aren't fitting together so nicely here. I'm hoping someone at the company might come forward. This is an inside job and it may take someone on the inside to help out."

"That'd make our jobs easier. Say, I was wondering if can you direct me to someone who works in Financial Crimes."

"Sure. They'd be over at the Parker Center, downtown. Guy to talk to is Mark Lutz. Why?"

"One thing is related to that Billy the Fixer. I want to get a little more info on him. But as far as Malco goes, don't worry. I've got someone from the inside trying to help out."

"Who's that?"

"I'd rather not say."

"Jesus Christ, Burnside! You still playing that Lone Ranger crap?"

"It's delicate," I shrugged. "But I'll keep you in the loop."

"You're a joy to work with, you know that?"

"I've been told worse."

"So now, anything else I can do for you? Maybe change the oil in your car?"

"No, Juan," I said, standing up to leave. "I'm good."

"Hey, you know you promised me some tickets to the UCLA game, remember? If I helped you out with the sting on Billy the Fixer? The game's coming up on Saturday and I already promised my kid. Am I getting those 50-yard line seats?"

I gulped. My last few days had been so full that this had slipped my mind. "I'm on it, Juan. I don't know the yard line yet. But I'm making progress."

Juan shook his head and went back to looking at his paperwork. "Yeah, progress," he said "I prefer results."

*

I returned to my office on Olympic Boulevard. The air felt a little musty inside, so I opened a window. A couple of high school girls sat at the bus stop bench staring vacantly into space. I checked voice mail and heard back from Amanda Hertz, who was able to get access to a vacant house we could use on the Westside. I took care of some busy work and also left a message for Johnny Cleary about Saturday's game.

With the sting coming up, I started doing some background work on Billy the Fixer. A quick search on the Internet revealed some interesting things. Amanda told me Billy was a thief, a con artist and a convicted felon. I now learned he was also an ordained minister. His church was one I had never heard of. Not really a surprise.

Billy's website was very professional and presented photos of smiling, muscular technicians working away. He wrote about the need to be energy-efficient and how that could save a customer money. He listed numerous references. I almost felt like having an air conditioning unit installed in my apartment. Fortunately, that's unnecessary in Santa Monica. More fortunately, I knew Billy was a wanted criminal and the cornucopia of technical information and pictures he displayed were most likely scraped from someone else's website.

The customer review sites on the Internet put forth an impression Billy had been installing HVAC systems very capably for years. Some people likely hired him because he had some good references. Then the reviews started turning negative. Customers posted that they had paid a deposit but he never finished the job. Or they paid for a new system and he installed one that was on its last legs. Interspersed in these complaints were a few glowing testimonials about how Billy was very honest and skillful, and how they were so glad they had hired him. I could only imagine the sermons he was preaching at his church.

I dialed the number on Billy's website. After four rings I heard an announcement that said they would be playing some music while they connected me. For the next 60 seconds I listened to a song by Cheap Trick, when all of a sudden there were a series of clicks and I heard a male voice.

"Hullo?"

"Is this Billy?"

"Who's this?" he said, answering the question with a question. Ah, so smart.

"My name's Jack. I saw some reviews of yours. We just bought a house and I need to get central air installed."

"Where do you live?"

I hesitated. Amanda's message didn't say where the property would be. But lying to a liar didn't seem to strike me as a problem. "Near Beverly Hills," I said. "Westside. Where are you located?"

"Oh I work all over," he said, the interest in his voice becoming more obvious. "In fact, I'm just finishing a job in Beverly Hills. Yeah, I'm installing the AC and heating in Kanye West's house. Huge job, he's got a mansion. But he loves our work. Do you know Kanye?"

I thought of saying we were neighbors but there's only so many lies I can tell before my tongue feels like it's about to snap off. "No, never met him," I said, but quickly added, "if you're doing work for Kanye you must be good."

"Oh hey, I'm the best," he spouted. "Why don't we set something up."

"Yeah, I'll need to check with my wife on our schedule," I said, needing to buy a little time for a small item like getting the address of our house. "When are you available?"

"Like I say, I'm finishing up in Beverly Hills. I'll be there the next few days. Just tell me when you want me to stop by and look things over."

We hung up and I called Mark Lutz at the Financial Crimes Division of the LAPD. I mentioned Juan Saavedra's name and he said he'd help me as much as he could. I asked him to check into Billy the Fixer, aka Billy Ray Fox. Lutz put me on hold and came back on the line a few minutes later.

"Yeah, you're right. We already have a warrant out on him for parole violations, but there's been half a dozen complaints filed for fraud. We're strapped on resources, and if he's not a violent offender, he's not the highest priority. Still, we don't turn our backs on this. If you have a way to collar him, let me know. We'll work with the prosecutor and put him away."

I thanked Mark for his help, and called Amanda back and left a message. Compared to the Malco case, this one felt almost too easy. Just then, my cell phone rang and the voice on the other end was a surprise.

"Burnside, this is Jason Chandler from Vegas Metro. I understand you were asking for me yesterday. Sorry it's taken a while to get back to you."

Today seemed like my lucky day for getting in touch with the men in blue. "Detective," I said. "Thanks for calling. Yes, I was hoping to get some help on a case. I understand you're acquainted with Kyle Otto."

"Big Kyle? Sure. I stop by for a pizza every now and then. Good guy. How do you know him?"

"We played football together at USC. Long time ago."

"Yeah, yeah," he exclaimed in an enthusiastic voice. "I remember you. Free safety, right? You were a big hitter if I recall."

"Still am, Detective."

"Ha! You know, I've been meaning to go by Kyle's place, haven't been there in a while. I'll ask about you."

I imagined whatever pizzas he was ordering would be on the house, but kept that little dig to myself. "I'm sure you're aware of the shooting at the Malco warehouse."

"Yeah, sorry you had to spend a lot of time here yesterday. Routine procedure, you know the drill."

"Understood. I've been through the wringer with Internal Affairs at LAPD. Never fun."

"Never fun," he repeated. "So is there something I can do for you?"

"As a matter of fact there is. There's a sports agent named Cliff Roper. I was wondering if you could check him out. He spends a lot of time in Vegas. Anything unusual, anything out of the ordinary."

"What's your interest in him?

"There's some possible violations going on. Related to the NCAA," I said, and then added, "it involves an SC football player. I'm trying to keep him out of trouble."

"That doesn't sound good. I still follow the Trojans up here. Big game coming up Saturday, huh?"

"Always a big one."

"Let me sniff around and see what I can find."

"Great, thanks. One other thing. Does the name Adam Barber mean anything to you?"

"Nope. Should it?"

"I don't know. I'd appreciate it if you could check him out, too. You never know."

"You never know. Hope that's all you got," he laughed. "I do have a day job here."

"That's it. Not unless you can get Kyle to deliver me a pizza tonight in Santa Monica."

Chandler laughed again and hung up. Amanda called me back and we set up a time later in the week to run the sting. When I told her I had spoken with Billy, she asked about every detail of the conversation. She asked if I was certain he was going to come, and I assured her he would be there. She gave me the address of the house, on a street called Sherbourne in the Pico-Robertson district. While it wasn't in Beverly Hills, it was about a mile or so away, close enough to get away with saying "Beverly Hills-adjacent. "

For Billy the Fixer, that should work out just fine.

Eleven

The next morning I headed back downtown, but this time my destination was more familiar. I had spent four years living down by USC and knew the area intricately. I pulled off the Santa Monica Freeway at Vermont Avenue and drove past the blighted thrift stores, auto repair shops, and taquerias. Most had iron bars protecting the windows, but a few retail outlets had a metal shutter pulled down over the full exterior, indicating they were closed, some of them for good.

The USC campus is situated in a large pocket near downtown L.A., and was now surrounded by gates and security entrances. Years ago, it was relatively easy to drive onto campus, and while you still can do so, there are now a host of restrictions. The university has had a good relationship with the nearby community, and during the 1992 uprising the campus went untouched despite looting and fires that destroyed businesses just blocks away.

Provost Hunt's office was located in the Bovard Administration Building. I showed up early enough that his assistant had yet to arrive. But at 7:30am, I knew the Provost would be well into his day.

"Good morning," I said, walking into his office. Provost Marshall Hunt looked up at me from his mug of coffee.

"And a good morning to you, sir!" he boomed, with an enthusiasm that belied his 63 years. "Why, I just got off the phone with an old chum from my days on the crew team at Harvard. And now you show up. I believe good things do come in bunches!"

"You're very kind," I smiled, marveling at his upbeat attitude. I regretted having to soon bring him back down to earth. "I do hope that's French roast. And I especially hope you aren't drinking the last cup."

Marshall Hunt laughed a hearty belly laugh. "You were never shy, were you? Not even when you were a student."

"Not then, not now."

"Please," he said, rising, his large girth moving surprisingly quickly to a counter which held a very fancy coffee maker. He pulled a white mug with a USC logo on it from a cabinet, filled it with coffee and handed it to me. He didn't bother to ask about cream or sugar, he seemed to remember I took it black.

"Thank you," I said, taking a sip. It may not have been French roast, but it was strong and robust and just what I needed. "I feel well taken care of."

"As a distinguished alumnus ought to!"

"I'm getting quite the royal treatment today."

"Yes, yes. But we do fawn over our stars. Johnny tells me you've been selected as honorary captain for the UCLA game. Congratulations. That's a wonderful honor."

"I'm thrilled. Honestly. And I've also been asked to address the team this week. Not sure what I'm going to say exactly. These kids are a lot more sophisticated than we were back in the day."

"It's a new world," he agreed. "But you'll do fine. You're one of the fellows we don't need to worry about."

"So I didn't realize the Provost got involved in matters outside academia."

Marshall Hunt smiled. "I like to help out where I can. And at this university, football is almost a religion. I'd be foolish to ignore it. Especially when it intertwines so deeply with our alumni base."

"Uh, yeah. Which brings me to why I stopped by."

Provost Hunt's jovial expression turned serious in the blink of an eye. "You mean Miles."

"Miles. His kids. The agent he was working with. A number of things are bubbling up to the surface."

The big man's face exuded concern. "Terrible thing about Miles. Tragic, absolutely tragic."

"Can you tell me anything more about him? I've heard he was a big donor to the university and he associated with some of the players. He seems to have had some connections with sports agents."

Marshall Hunt sighed. "Miles and Clara certainly were generous, yes. But that was a while back. The past couple of years they haven't been donating. Oh, it's hardly an issue, everyone has their ups and downs. But I understand their business isn't as lucrative as it had been years ago."

"Any idea as to what happened?"

"Not really. But we did take notice that Miles was very friendly with a few of the agents. And while we do our best to keep the agents and their runners away from the players, these fellows continue to reach them. Sometimes through the alumni. We've started to close off football practice to outsiders -- which was naturally a problem for the agents. Miles, of course, was not an outsider, and he had access."

"So he was making some introductions."

"And I'd heard he had an understanding with the agents that if a player signed with them, Miles would get a commission. Ordinarily there isn't that strong a link between an agent and a donor. But when people get into financial trouble you'd be surprised at some of the levels they sink to."

"Does the name Cliff Roper ring a bell?"

"Oh yes. He's signed a few of our kids, a couple are still active in the NFL. And Cliff's one of the reasons we had to cordon off practice. Very aggressive fellow. He'd march right up to the players after practice and practically give them a five-hundred dollar handshake. We absolutely can't allow that and try to keep them away from the team. But they have runners who manage to ingratiate themselves. No matter what we tell the players, a few will forget."

"Do you have any contact info for Roper?"

"I can get it for you. I'm not sure talking with him will help."

"Maybe I can get through," I mused.

"Are there any players he's approached lately?"

"You really want to know the answer to that?"

The Provost smiled a knowing smile. "Perhaps not."

"By the way, since we're on this subject of players and agents. Were Miles' kids involved with any of this?"

"No, not that I could tell. Peter and Isabelle come to a few alumni events, but I think they were mostly focused on running the business. I'm sure they're quite nervous about the future after what happened this weekend. And speaking of which, do the police have any leads?"

I shook my head. "Nothing concrete. They have a few

people they're looking at, a couple of employees who have had issues in the past, but none have a good motive. Taking out Miles wasn't going to change anything for them."

"Nasty situation. I spoke with Clara yesterday, gave her my condolences. If you speak with her, please let her know the university will help her in any way we can."

I thanked him for his time and left the Provost to get on with his day. Walking over to the student union building, I wandered through the early morning dining options before settling in at a coffee kiosk for my second cup of the day. Back when I was a student, there was a cafeteria that served watery coffee and a few menu selections and that was it. Today, a sizeable food court had been built, and there was a wide plethora of choices.

As I started to ponder how I got from being a wide-eyed student athlete to becoming a world weary private investigator, my phone began to buzz. The 702 area code told me Vegas was calling. Maybe, just maybe, I'd hit the jackpot.

"Good morning."

"This Burnside?"

"It is."

"Hey, it's Chandler. Listen I got something on a one Cliff Roper for you."

"Anything good?"

"Oh you have no idea. This Roper used to live here, he's a piece of work. He's been booked on check kiting, forgery, wire fraud, bank fraud. He even got charged with manslaughter."

"A real winner, I see. And he's still walking around free as a bird."

"Hey, with a good lawyer a guy can get away with a lot. Even murder. I've seen it."

"Me too," I said. "Tell me about the manslaughter charge."

"Business dispute with a partner. These things happen with guys who move in certain circles. But he got off, hung jury. They tried him three times before throwing in the towel. The prosecutor here wanted to try him for jury rigging too, but he didn't have enough hard evidence."

"Let me guess. The partner had something to do with a sports agency."

"You'd guess right. That was before he changed his name of course."

"Do what?"

"He used to be Hal Delano. Now he's Cliff Roper. Legally changed his name. Isn't America a great country?"

"Guess that was good for business."

"I told you he was a piece of work. I'll bet there's a few football players who haven't heard about this stuff."

"Probably not," I said. "But there's bound to be a few who like the gangster aspect."

"Sure. And he's certainly not the first agent to have criminal charges brought against him. But like I said, a good lawyer can work wonders."

"This is pretty eye-opening stuff. Thank you."

"Yeah. I hope you're able to help that player. At the very least keep him away from Hal. Or Cliff. Or whatever he's calling himself these days."

"And anything regarding the other name I gave you? Adam Barber?"

"No, nothing. But when I came across this, I figured I'd give you a call right away. If I find out anything, I'll call you."

"Thanks. If you ever need a favor, let me know. I owe you."

"I'll remember that," he laughed and hung up. Thankfully he didn't ask for tickets to the UCLA game.

*

Cliff Roper's offices were located in Hollywood in a high rise building near the corner of Sunset and Vine. This was not the Hollywood of decades past, where the tired boulevards and tawdry shops were far beyond their heyday. A *cappuccino* bar and a few trendy eateries were stationed at the bottom floor of the building. I shook my head as I noticed one that had a sign in their window advertising they only served grilled cheese sandwiches. I rode the elevator up to the 25th floor and walked out onto the deep, plush carpeting. The glass enclosed offices were inscribed with the name Roper Sports and a logo featuring a lightning bolt.

I walked inside and came upon a lovely young woman with long blonde hair and a low cut top. She smiled a glittery smile and asked how she could help me.

"You look very familiar," I said in my most charming voice. "Have you been on TV?"

"Actually yes. I used to be a cheerleader with the Seahawks. I'm from Seattle."

"Nice place when it's not raining."

"Oh, you know what they say. If you don't like the weather in Seattle, just wait five minutes."

"Are you down here to make it as an actor?"

She smiled the big smile. "That's the plan."

"Good one. I'm sure you'll do great. Say, could I see Cliff for a minute?"

"Sure. What's your name?"

"Vince Lombardi. I'm an old friend. Okay if I go in?"

"Gee ... I'm supposed to announce you," she started.

"You can tell him I'm coming in. Don't want to give him too much notice. It's a surprise."

"Um, I guess."

She picked up the phone and spoke briefly into it. I wandered past her desk and walked down a corridor. When I came to the corner office with his name on it, I turned the handle and walked in.

Cliff Roper was a very short, wiry man in his early 50s with graying hair. He wore an expensive suit and had on a black shirt with the top two buttons open. Even as he was sitting at his desk I could tell he was short, but when he put down the phone and stood up, he removed all doubt. He was probably no taller than 5' 3".

"Okay. Who the fuck are you? And don't give me that Vince Lombardi crap."

"Your cupcake out there seemed to buy it."

"Yeah well I'm not her. Start talking or get out."

I approached him. "My name's Burnside."

"And that's supposed to mean something?"

I laughed. "And to think you're in the sports business."

"State your case, man. I don't have all day."

"I'm a private investigator," I said slowly. "I was hired by Miles Larson. That name ring a bell?"

Roper froze. He nodded and told me to go on. I noticed he didn't invite me to sit down. Such poor manners.

"You know Miles is dead."

"No shit, Sherlock. I read the papers. What's that got to do with me?"

"You and he had some business dealings. Heard it wasn't going smoothly."

"You heard wrong. I didn't have a problem with Miles."

"You've got one with Marcellus Williams, though. And now you're going to have one with me."

Cliff sneered at me. "Who the hell are you? And why should I care? Look, get to the point or get out."

I resolved not to suggest that the point was on top of his head. "How many of your players know about your criminal record? How many know you've changed your name, Hal? Does the NFL Players Association know about any of this?"

Cliff stopped sneering. His mouth opened briefly, but nothing came out. When an agent is at a loss for words, you know you've made an impact. I became certain of it when he offered me a chair. He closed the door and we sat down at a round oak table by the window. The view was of Beachwood Canyon, and the Hollywood sign was close by. It was a little smoggy, but the visibility wasn't bad. It could have been worse.

"Tell me what you know," he said slowly.

"I don't know everything, but I know a lot. And what I know *can* hurt you," I replied.

"What do you want from me?"

"For starters, back off of Marcellus Williams. Stop trying to blackmail him."

David Chill

Roper smirked. "Is that what this is about? Some kid from the hood sent you to threaten me?"

"Is that a problem for you? Is that worth blowing your small empire?"

"Man, how do you think we make a living here? Megawatt signs with me and he's got no problems. He plays college ball until he's eligible for the pros. Then we both make a lot of money."

"I don't think you're listening to me."

"Look, this kid is solid gold. MW is going to be worth a hundred million by the time his career is done. I'm taking a piece of that," he declared, and then he looked straight at me. "Okay. How much do you want? I'll give you a cut up front."

"That's not why I'm here," I said, wondering if English was his first language. "If you're going to sign Marcellus, you can do it in two years. Until then you keep your distance."

"Do I hear an or-else at the end of that?"

"What do you think would happen to your agent certification if the NFL Players Association learned you were indicted for bank fraud and wire fraud?"

"They'd think I was innocent until proven guilty," he countered. "Last I heard this was the United States of Kiss My Ass."

"And what if you were arrested for the murder of Miles Larson?"

Roper stared at me. "You got any proof of that?"

"Maybe there's enough proof to put the police on your tail."

"What proof?"

"Does it matter? Once the news is out that you're being

158

investigated for murder, I think it's possible someone just might leak some of those other things about your background. You might think your clients'll admire you for being a tough guy. They won't admire you for stealing from your other clients. They'll be worried it might happen to them."

"They won't leave me," he insisted, attempting a certain level of bluster. I noticed he took a hard swallow.

"You want to take that risk? You're a businessman. You know that it's a whole lot cheaper to keep your existing clients than to try and get new ones."

He shook his head. "You're doing all this for Megawatt? What'd he ever do for you?"

It was a good question, and I paused for a moment. It was hard to explain Trojan Family to an outsider. "Call it a favor to his coach."

Roper's eyes narrowed. "Maybe I could back off," he said, his mouth curled. "Then again, maybe you might disappear."

I stared back at him for a long moment and then zipped open my jacket wide enough to reveal the .38 in its nylon ballistic holster. After his wide eyes confirmed he had seen it, I zipped up the jacket again.

"Don't bring your goons out," I warned him. "They won't stand a chance. And remember, there's other people who know what I know. Anything happens to me, and everything about you gets released. And everything is what you stand to lose."

Roper slumped back in his chair. "You got stones. I'll give you that."

"One more thing."

"What? You want something else now?"

"What's your relationship with Eddie Larson?"

Roper shook his head. "Business associate. Kind of like Miles only different. They help me get clients."

"How are they different?"

"I've known Eddie for years. He introduced me to Miles. Miles made the introductions to the players. Eddie helps close the deals. Both get their cuts."

"And everyone's happy."

"Yeah. Except when some private eye sticks his nose where it doesn't belong."

"You have your interests, I have mine. Do we have an agreement?"

"About what?"

"About your leaving Marcellus Williams alone for the next two years. You can sign him when he's eligible to go to the NFL. Not before. Or else ... "

Roper looked off into the distance. "Okay. I'll wait for him. Jesus. I feel like a fucking broad. I'll wait for him."

I rose and didn't bother to stick out my hand. "Appreciate your seeing my side of this."

"Yeah. I can't tell you how happy I am you stopped by."

Twelve

I headed back to my office and thought about my speech to the football team. Johnny wanted me to address the squad and give them a pep talk. We had alums come in when I was a player. Some elderly guy would tell us about the good old days, which typically evoked widespread fidgeting and watch checking. But every once in a while, a former player would be remarkably captivating and would make us listen to them. What they said felt important at the time. I wanted to be one of those guys.

My phone rang as I was parking my Pathfinder. As I glanced down, I saw the call was from a blocked number. I wavered briefly as to whether or not to answer it. I had come to hate telemarketers and even though it was illegal, they still would call my cell phone number. But I was feeling good this morning, things were on a roll. I decided to pick up. It turned out to be a good move.

"Hey Burnside, it's Chase. Remember me?"

"I remember. The installer extraordinaire."

"Huh?" he asked.

"Never mind. What's up?

"I need to talk to you. I heard you're a detective, not a consultant."

"Yeah. At the time I couldn't tell anyone outside the family what I was doing."

"Uh-huh. Hey, I'm wondering if I could talk to you. In person, you know."

"Sure. Want me to meet you at Malco?"

"No. Anywhere but there. Hey, I'm on the Westside now. Where are you?"

"Westside, also. Why don't you swing by my office."

I gave him my address and walked upstairs. There was a pile of unsorted mail that needed tending to, and the property manager had slipped a note under the door asking when I'd be paying this month's rent. I plopped down into my chair and waited to see what Chase wanted. I was no closer to learning who was stealing from Malco, and no closer to learning who killed Miles. But at least I put some separation between Marcellus and his would-be agent, Roper. So the day was off to a good start.

Chase walked into my office a little while later and looked around. "Hey there. You work out of this place, huh?"

"Not exactly opulent is it? Anyway, I don't need a fancy office."

"Sure. Hey listen, I'm wondering how things are coming along with finding the guy who did Miles."

"I don't think the police have much. And don't be so positive it's a guy. You never know."

Chase gave a dry laugh. "Yeah. You never know, huh."

I looked at him. "Do you know anything about it?"

Chase sat down and twisted the end of his thick moustache. He pondered the question for just a little too long.

"Anything you can share would be helpful," I added.

"I don't know who did it," he finally said. "But I think I might be able to help."

It was my turn to ponder things for a moment. "Why aren't you taking this to the police?" I finally asked.

"They've been pushing me lately for what I might know," he admitted. "And I may be in some trouble."

My eyebrows shot up. "How's that?"

Chase shook his head. Hard. "It's not what you think. Not exactly. I had nothing to do with Miles' murder. I can guarantee you that. But I don't want to go to the police because ... hey, it's complicated."

"Maybe I can help simplify things."

"I dunno. Look, a while ago I helped Miles out of a jam. He got into an argument one morning with one of the installers. Real weirdo. The guy accused Miles of cheating him out of his money. It was early in the morning and not a lot of people had shown up yet."

"Where did this argument happen?"

"Miles' office. The weirdo went in there and started threatening Miles. Said he was being dinged because of a bad score on one of those customer surveys. I was down the hall getting some coffee when I heard some loud voices. I walked over and saw the two of them fighting. I ran in and pulled the weirdo off of Miles. I had my arms wrapped around the guy."

"Go on," I said.

"That's when Miles started beating on him. Really laid into the guy. For an old dude, Miles could pack a punch."

"So you held him and Miles kept hitting him."

"Hey, it wasn't exactly like that. But yeah, close. I tried to jerk the guy around and put my body between him and Miles. But Miles, he wouldn't have any of that. I told him to go easy, but Miles pulled out a pipe and really started to go to town on the guy. I finally had to let the guy go and grab Miles. Else he would've killed him."

I tried to take this all in. "So the fight ended. What happened to that installer?"

"Spent a few weeks in the hospital. When he got out he filed assault charges against Miles. Also filed some kind of personal lawsuit for a million dollars or something."

"Did it go to court? Something tells me Miles wasn't going to settle something like that."

"Hell no he wasn't," Chase agreed. "In fact that's where it got tricky for me."

"Why? You were just trying to be the peacemaker. A good Samaritan."

"That's not how Miles was going to present it to the police. He told me if I didn't cooperate and take his side, he'd tell the police I was part of the assault."

"His word against yours."

"Not exactly," he said. "You see Miles had a video recording of the fight. And when he played it back to me, it looked like I was holding the guy while he belted him. He had the sound turned off, and just looking at the video image, a judge could easily think I was in on the assault."

"Okay, but you weren't. Why wouldn't you just tell the truth?"

Chase stared down at the ground. "Look, I'm not proud of stuff I've done. But I need this job. Bad. I'm in debt up to my eyeballs. I owe a lot of money and Miles said if I didn't play ball, I'd be fired. And he guaranteed that I'd never work anywhere in this business again."

"I don't know that that's true. You're a good installer, you can get other gigs somewhere. It's not like Miles owns the world."

"Hey, he figured out he could own me. I also have a criminal record. Got into some trouble a while back. I have two felonies on my record. A third one and I go away for a long time, that's what the judge warned me about. Didn't seem like he was messing around."

"And Miles threatened to show the recording to the police if you didn't back him up."

"That's right. I didn't like it, but Miles said not to feel bad, the guy got what was coming to him. And after that, Miles treated me pretty good. I had some trouble working with his kids, they wanted to fire me. On account I objected to some of their great ideas, like taking away our lunch breaks. I was pretty vocal about it. Miles obviously didn't agree with me, but he made them back off. It was like he appreciated my stepping up to help him."

I sat back and took all of this in. Chase was telling me this story for a reason. He wasn't about to bare his soul to a relative stranger unless there was something more. I had a funny feeling what that was.

"Tell me about the video recording. How'd he do it?"

Chase looked me dead in the eye for a long second. "Yeah. So the thing is, Miles had a video camera set up in his office. It was hidden inside that USC helmet on the shelf. No one knew it was there. He showed me the setup later, it was in a small storage room next to Miles' office. You wouldn't even know it was there, it was so well disguised. He put it in himself. I guess when he first started the business, he used to do some installing too. Back in the day. Said he wanted to make sure he had some video proof in case one of the union guys decided to blackmail him. Man, was Miles paranoid about that union."

"And did he record everything?"

"I think he did. He told me he had set it up to be voice-activated."

"But you said the sound was turned down on the recording of the fight, didn't you?"

"Yeah, Miles said he removed the audio just so the police wouldn't hear that I was trying to break it up. I guess he was a pretty good technician himself."

"Okay," I said slowly. "So if Miles recorded everything ... "

" ... Then he recorded what happened to him last Saturday morning." Chase said, finishing my thought.

"And no one else knows this?"

Chase shook his head no. "Miles was adamant about that. He said no one could know or I'd be fired and he'd hand me over to the police. He only told me about his video system because he had to. So if anyone did find out, he'd know it would've had to come from me."

"I imagine you could show me how to access these videos," I said.

"Yeah," he said. "But it's not gonna be easy. We can't just march in there without drawing suspicion. And I don't want the police to find everything, because I could be in some hot water."

"I have an idea," I said. "What time does the office close at night?"

"I dunno. Everyone's usually gone by about 8:00pm. But security's tight now. You know."

"Leave that to me. I've got a plan. Can you meet me at Malco tonight at say, 8:30?"

"I can do that," he agreed.

"And you'd want something in return."

"Yeah," he said. "You can guess what that is."

"Because eventually someone is bound to discover the video equipment. And they might find that recording of the fight with you and Miles and that other installer."

"Might be good if I was the only one who had a copy of that."

Chase was shrewd. And smart. He had something to trade and there was something he wanted. At least I knew what I was dealing with.

"Okay," I told him. "I can live with that. You're going out on a limb here. You won't have a problem."

Chase stood up. "I still don't see how we're going to get into that room."

"We private eyes have our ways," I said and smiled. "One thing you might want to do though."

"What's that?"

"Wear a baseball cap and pull it down low to cover your face. I'll be able to justify why I'm there, but I think we want to keep your identity shrouded, in case we don't find what we're looking for. And I'm not about to spray paint any cameras."

*

I spent the rest of the afternoon trying to think about tomorrow's speech to the team, but my thoughts kept drifting towards what might be on that video recording at Malco. I checked in with Gail, and she excitedly told me she was called for an interview with the L.A. City Attorney. It wasn't as prestigious as working for the U.S. Attorney's office, but it was here, it was home, and most importantly she said, it was near me. I smiled into the phone as I listened to her gush about the possibilities.

This being November, it had grown dark before 6:00pm. The night was clear and cool, and the moon was nearly full as I headed down the Harbor Freeway and exited east onto Florence Avenue. The well traveled boulevard leading up to Malco was brightly lit, but once I turned down the side street where their office stood, the street lights grew dim. The silver glow of the moon guided my path, and I pulled into a space near the front of the building.

There was one other car in the parking lot, a Toyota sedan with a red, temporary handicapped placard hanging from the rear view mirror. A car in the parking lot didn't always mean someone was inside. People sometimes left their cars at work overnight, especially if they were on a business trip. Or if they planned a romantic interlude with a colleague, and didn't care who knew. The possibilities were endless. A plain white Econoline van pulled up next to me a few minutes later, and the engine idled until I got out of my vehicle.

"Hey," Chase said, in what was probably his standard greeting. He got out of his van and I noticed he was wearing a bright red Angels baseball cap. He had pulled the long visor down low. I always liked it when people followed my directions.

"Hey yourself," I replied. "You ready?"

"Oh yeah," he nodded. "I can't wait to see what we find. Or how you're going to get us in there."

"I have a plan," I said. "My only concern is avoiding the security guard."

Chase scoffed. "He goes to bed early. He's probably dozing in the warehouse."

"Okay. Follow me," I said, and waved him forward. As we approached the front entrance of Malco, I reached into my pocket and pulled out two pairs of latex gloves, and handed one pair to Chase. Better safe than sorry. If we didn't find any evidence, it would be hard to explain why he were here. I removed the consultant's badge that Miles had arranged for me to have. Waving it in front of the security pad, I heard a series of clicks and grabbed the handle of the door. I pulled it open and we walked inside to the lobby. Another wave in front of a new pad allowed us access to the interior of the office.

We walked down the quiet hallways, past the sea of empty cubicles. Some auxiliary lighting was turned on near the baseboards, providing plenty of light to see, but still maintaining an atmosphere that was dim to the point of being almost romantic. As we approached Miles' corner office, I turned to Chase.

"Okay. Where is this secret room?"

"We have to go through Miles' office first."

I waved my badge in front of the pad, but this time there were no clicks. No sound at all was emitted. It was as if an expensive toy had just broken at the single worst time. I pressed it hard against the flat surface this time, but again, no response. And then all of a sudden, I heard a rustling sound nearby. I whirled around the corner and came face-to-face with a short, stocky woman pushing a trash bin. We stared at each other briefly.

"*Hola*," I finally managed, in what had to have come off as a surprised voice.

"It is okay," she said. "I speak English."

I paused for a second. "That's good because *Hola* is about all the Spanish I know."

She giggled. "You are working late."

"Yes," I said and held out my badge. "I can't seem to access this office. Can you help?"

"Oh," she hesitated. "I think the police wanted to keep this closed off."

I pulled out my wallet containing my private investigator's license. I had enhanced it with a thick golden shield for moments like these.

"I'm a detective," I said, placing the shield directly in front of her, and holding up my hands to display the latex gloves. "We're not looking to disturb the crime scene, we're here to gather some additional evidence. We didn't want to come in during the day when everyone was working. This is very sensitive."

"Oh, you mean like in CSI?"

I nodded solemnly. "Exactly."

"Ah, I suppose. You will lock up when you leave?"

"Sure," I said.

"Tonight the night people are working late," she commented. "Usually only janitors here."

I looked at Chase and then back at the woman. "Who else is working late?"

The woman shrugged. We looked down the hall and all the office doors were closed. Whoever was here seemed to want as much privacy as we did.

"What do you think?" asked Chase.

"We're here," I said. "As long as we're quiet and keep the door closed, we should be fine. If not, we'll deal with it. I'm used to improvising."

The woman reached into her apron, pulled out a badge and waved it in front of the pad. A second later there was a magical click and we entered Miles' office. I thanked the janitor and closed the door behind us. Once safely ensconced inside, I picked up a chair and leaned it against the door to prevent any other entrants.

Chase led me to a door which opened into what looked like a walk-in closet. As we entered, he walked to the far side and jimmied a handle sticking out near the ceiling. All of a sudden the wall turned into a sliding door, which was fortunately bereft of a security pad. It opened into a small, wood-paneled room containing shelves of electronic equipment. Different colored LED lights were blinking furiously on one wall, a display that reminded me of a command station in an old James Bond film.

"This is Miles' surveillance room," said Chase.

I looked around. A different wall contained a series of

small TV monitors mounted next to one another. The room contained exactly one chair. I looked at Chase. "He spies on his employees?"

Chase shrugged. "It's a small business. I've heard he monitored people's phone calls, too."

"Do you think Peter and Isabelle know about this?"

"Doubt it. Like I told you, Miles said I was the only other person who knew. Me and Miles. Now you, of course."

"This is amazing," I remarked, as I looked around the small room in awe. "And you think you can find the recording we need?"

Chase gave a derisive laugh. "This isn't high school A/V. I'm a video technician. If it's here, I'll find it."

We sat down and I spent the next two and a half hours watching Chase sift through an assortment of archived videos ranging from the monotonous to the mundane. Some were logged by date, others by title, and some had no label at all. There was no particular order for how the footage was stored.

Chase finally discovered the video showing he and Miles roughing up the installer who challenged Miles. And about 10 minutes later, he came across the final video of Miles Larson's storied business career. We watched it in silent shock, listened to the conversation that played out in a bizarre manner, and then glanced at one another in disbelief.

"Okay," I managed. "It's rough to see someone murdered in cold blood like that. But we have to show it to the police. Can you do a few downloads of that one onto some DVDs?"

"Yeah," he said blankly, and began to play with the equipment. After a few minutes he handed me the disks I needed, and then pocketed the one with himself in it. Chase put everything back so it appeared to be the way we originally found it. We then got up to leave. Walking out of the ancillary room, we stopped and looked at Miles' office one last time.

"Hell of a way to go, huh?" he said.

"Just when you think you've seen it all."

"Good thing the audio was working. Sometimes the images tell only part of the story."

I glanced over at the cardinal USC helmet, still situated on a shelf, and most likely still working. "Funny how things play themselves out," I said. "Miles set this up with no idea he'd be recording his own murder."

Chase looked over at it. "Suppose I should de-activate the camera?"

"No need at this point," I said. "Once I hand the DVD over, the police will know we've been through here. Besides, we're not the ones with anything to hide."

The lock on Miles' office door clicked a moment after we walked out. I slipped the DVDs into my jacket pocket and we walked through the lobby and out the front door. The night had grown considerably cooler and I was glad I wore my jacket. But as we turned to go into the parking lot, a deep male voice boomed.

"Hold it right there you two!"

We looked up and stood face-to-face with a tanned man with a head of thinning, silver hair. The head of security at Malco was waiting for us. Glen Butterworth had a malevolent expression on his face and a chrome plated 9mm Beretta in his hand.

Thirteen

The night air was chilly and silent. The three of us stood motionless as we surveyed the scene. While Chase had no business entering Miles' office, I did have security clearance and had been hired by the widow of the company founder to do an investigation. Chase's reason for being here was more vague, but I could justify it by saying he was assisting me in the investigation. But when someone is pointing a gun at you, logic and reason take a back seat to sidling out of the immediate dilemma.

"I'd be a little careful with where you're pointing that thing," I started.

"And I'd stop giving me directives if I were you," Butterworth replied, in that baritone voice I now fully despised.

"What are you doing here?" I asked.

"I think I'll ask you the same question," he said, pointing the gun menacingly. "And you go first."

"Okay. Clara hired us to investigate. This is part of the investigation."

"At 11:00 at night? Just what kind of an investigator are you?"

The kind that doesn't like guns pointed at him, I thought. "This is when my business gets done," I said, trying to deflect things.

"And what did you find out tonight?"

"Nothing worth knowing," I lied, getting nervous about the DVDs in my pocket. "What brings you here?"

"I'm the head of security, asshole. I got an alert that someone came through the front door after hours. My guard said he combed through the building, but the lazy ass couldn't find anyone. But there was also no indication that anyone had left. I just came down and waited. Figured you wouldn't spend the night in there."

"Cagey," I mused. "Too bad we didn't find anything."

"You were in there for almost three hours. That's a lot of time spent to find nothing."

I shrugged. "Some nights are better than others."

"And this one's going to get worse for you. If you want to see tomorrow, you better start talking."

My mind raced. Deflect as much as possible. "I told you about the thefts going on in Vegas. And Adam Barber. All that should be pretty easy to stop."

Butterworth grinned. "And why would I want to stop that?"

A long period of silence passed, as the moment of clarity began to settle in. "I didn't know you were part of this," I said, choosing my words carefully.

"Yeah, you're a great detective, aren't you?"

"Of course I wouldn't have thought Isabelle would be stealing from her own father."

Butterworth paused and seemingly began to recalculate. "Oh so you figured that out, huh? How'd you do that?"

"I didn't. I took a shot. You just confirmed it."

"What?! The hell I did. Just what do you think you know?"

"This part all makes sense now," I told him. "You and Isabelle have been having an affair. I guess you didn't realize that's an open secret around here. The company is losing money. The two of you cooked up a scheme to steal merchandise. You run operations, she runs finance. Your crew wheels the product out the back door like it's trash, so no one suspects anything. The product is then sold off. Isabelle cooks the books so no one can figure it out."

Butterworth stared at me. "Maybe you're not so dumb after all."

"What's Peter's involvement here?"

"Peter?" he scoffed. "He's an idiot. A sycophant. He thinks he'll inherit a profitable company. He has no idea what shape it's in. Isabelle knew. Miles knew. Peter just sees what he wants to see."

"And Eddie?"

He hesitated for a moment. "Eddie's a free agent. He's separated from the business. Oh he thinks he'll get his share one day. But there won't be anything left by then."

"Because you'll have taken it all."

Butterworth laughed. "You still don't get it, do you? This company is being bled dry by the cable company. They pay less and less and demand more and more. There's a reason cable companies have stopped using their own installers. They can hire outside third parties like Malco and then work them to the bone and cut their rates each year. Malco is like a dead man walking. Peter just doesn't know it yet."

"So you're just getting your share while you can."

"Yeah," he sneered. "I'm a businessman. That's what we do. Get our share."

"You have an interesting definition of business," I said, trying to keep talking and distract him for as long as I could. When a criminal starts to acknowledge his crimes, it's often a prelude to killing someone. Thieves sometimes have a need to talk, not necessarily because they have a conscious desire to get caught, but rather to demonstrate how smart they think they are. The ones with consciences probably do have a deep seated need to be found out and punished. But the criminal world is loaded with sociopaths, unburdened by any sense of guilt. Understanding whether or not you had a sociopath on your hands could not be determined in a five-minute conversation.

"Look, I've worked in security for almost 30 years," he said. "I've seen it all. You wouldn't believe the type of crooked enterprises I've been around. Some of the most clean cut people you'd ever want to meet are ripping off their customers left and right."

"And did you just decide to join them now?" I said.

"Uh-huh. Yeah. This place was a dream. Ripe for the picking. Old man who founded the company is still there, maybe losing his edge. Idiot son's been anointed as the next CEO when his father dies. Middle aged daughter desperate for love, willing to partake in a scheme. The company still had good cash flow, but profits were shrinking to the point where Malco would soon be a house of cards. Oh yeah. This place was perfect."

"How did murder get mixed up in this?"

He gave me a funny look. "Just what do you know about what happened to Miles?"

"I know who did it."

Butterworth's mouth hung open for a minute. The thought that I had learned who killed Miles was too juicy to leave untouched. Butterworth stopped for a moment before figuring out his next move. I thought if I could lead Butterworth inside the building, I'd have a chance to turn the tables on him.

"Tell me," he said.

"You know, life can be full of surprises," I said. "This one definitely surprised me."

"Right. So who did it?"

"You wouldn't believe it. I'll need to show you. The evidence is inside," I said, my mind whirring with thoughts. I needed to get him inside. "It's in Isabelle's office."

Butterworth stared at me. "Okay. Let's go. You guys first."

He motioned for Chase and I to start moving towards the building. As we approached the front entrance I stopped and looked at him.

"My badge doesn't work anymore," I lied, "we'll need to use yours."

Butterworth pulled his badge from his back pocket and waved it in front of the pad. I made no move at this point, but raised my arms to chest level and kept them that way. The door unlocked and we walked back in, moving down the long hallway towards Isabelle's office. As we approached, Chase and I stepped aside for Butterworth to unlock Isabelle's door, too. Stepping forward, he was now to the left of me, but kept the gun nestled in his right hand. They say all criminals make at least one mistake, and this was his. He stopped paying attention for a moment. He let his guard down. He assumed that because I had not tried anything at the front entrance then I wouldn't try anything here. And there are few mistakes worse than assuming.

Butterworth gave me only a sideways glance as he waved his badge in front of the pad next to Isabelle's door. He pointed the gun directly at me but his eyes were focused on unlocking the door. And as the badge yielded another click, he reached for the handle. At that moment I slammed my left hand down on his right forearm. Grabbing the arm tightly, I jammed it downward so the gun was facing the floor. I then jerked his body back a step and drove my right foot solidly into his groin. He yelped in pain and doubled over. I yanked the gun out of his hand and took three steps backwards.

And at that point, the door to Isabelle's office swung wide open and someone emerged from Isabelle's office. Quickly surveying the scene, Sal Valdez glanced at Butterworth and then back at me.

"What's going on here?" he asked.

"Long story," I responded.

At this point, Butterworth began to straighten back up, although the look of agony was still on his face. "You guys aren't getting away with this," he said hoarsely. "You're in deep shit."

Sal took an unsteady step towards him. "From what I've learned, I think it is you who will have the problem. A really big problem."

Butterworth mouth curled into a snarl. "You can go to hell! God damn spic bastard!"

And with that, Sal Valdez raised his black cane to shoulder level and swung it angrily at Butterworth's face. The blow hit him across the cheek and Butterworth spun around before falling to one knee, and starting to moan.

"That's a really sweet swing," I observed.

"I used to play baseball."

"What's that thing made of?"

"Solid hickory. It's called the Bad Ass cane. I use it because of my hip. But look, this is a rough neighborhood. You never know when you might need some help."

I shook my head and laughed. The last place you'd think you need a blunt instrument is in the hallway of your own workplace. The last person you'd think you'd need to use it on is the guy in charge of security. Taking a glance over at Chase for the first time however, I saw he was far from laughing. In fact, during the whole episode, Chase did not utter a single word. I wasn't even certain he drew in a breath.

"Are you okay?" I asked.

"Jesus," he gulped. "How did you have a normal conversation with someone holding a gun on you?"

I shrugged. "Experience I guess."

*

The police arrived shortly after we dialed 911. Chase asked if he could leave and we just pretend he hadn't been there, but I reminded him that Butterworth or Valdez would probably let it slip. I told Chase he had nothing to worry about. He was an employee of Malco and it's not a crime to enter your place of employment, even if it's after hours. And there were going to be far bigger problems to deal with at this company.

In the few minutes before the police showed up, we moved outside and I went over and locked the DVDs in the glove compartment of my Pathfinder; Chase hid his in his van. Juan Saavedra and Roberto DeSanto were going to be the first ones to look at my DVD evidence. I didn't want it being handled by the midnight shift. We had worked too long and too hard to get this, and I wasn't going to risk it moving into hands I did not know. I talked briefly with Chase and we agreed to be as vague as possible, we were here looking for evidence in the investigation and found nothing. Chase was with me because he knew where things were in the building. Valdez was working late, and that was one aspect we wouldn't need to fudge.

"Sal," I said, before the police arrived, "just what *were* you doing in Isabelle's office?"

"Actually I was doing some work for you, *señor*," he answered.

"Me? What work was that?"

"Looking through some of her financial statements. I found a lot of things that don't line up. Bank statements that don't match the internal documents. Emails to and from Butterworth that point to collusion and embezzlement, among other things. I imagine they'll need to go through her computer to find out the whole stinking mess."

I frowned. "If she gets wind of what happened tonight she may race down here and grab her computer."

Valdez smiled. "No worries, *señor*," he said, and patted his briefcase. "I got that taken care of."

"Maybe you should put that in your trunk before the night shift gets here," I suggested. "There's a fine line between gathering evidence and employee theft. And we want to make sure all this gets into the proper hands."

Valdez agreed and walked to his vehicle. Without Juan Saavedra, there might be some sticky issues when the LAPD arrived. A private eye and two middling employees roughing up a seemingly respectable corporate executive would be enough to give any police officer pause. I pulled out my phone and called Juan's home number. It rang four times before a groggy voice on the other end said hello.

"Juan, it's Burnside."

"Oh, cripes."

"Yeah, I know. Everyone loves to hear from me, especially around midnight."

"This better be good."

"It's very good. The Larson murder case is going to be closed soon."

"Oh yeah?" he said in a far more alert voice. "Tell me more."

"I think I'll need to show you. Trust me, it's worth it. I can come in tomorrow."

"Crap. I'm tied up at the Parker Center most of the day. Can you stop by around five?"

"That's fine. But I, uh, got a situation here. Could use your help."

A loud sigh filled the phone. "Now what?"

"I needed access to Malco's headquarters. Getting in was no problem. Getting out had some unforeseen complications. Let's just say, the head of security wasn't very happy to see me."

"At a quarter to twelve at night, who would be?"

"Uh, yeah. His name's Glen Butterworth. He was part of the ring. We have a confession on grand theft, and there's going to be more on him."

"You didn't beat it out of him, did you?"

"No, but there was, ah, a slight altercation when I needed to take his gun away from him. But he actually bragged about what he had done. Pride is one of the seven deadly sins."

"Just what I wanted to hear right now," he sighed.

"No problem. In fact, the six other sins stem from pride."

"Jesus. I need to get a lecture here? All right. I'll make a couple of calls and keep you out of trouble for a day. But what you show me better be damn good."

I put the phone back in my pocket and we waited for the initial LAPD cruiser to show up. The first uniforms to arrive were a pair of Hispanic officers, and Sal Valdez immediately greeted them in Spanish. They spoke for what seemed like five minutes before returning to their patrol car and calling for backup. Butterworth tried yelling for them to arrest us, but they simply told him to be quiet. Within a few minutes there were a half dozen police cars spread out in the parking lot, and I knew we'd be in for a long night.

It took about three hours to get everyone's statements. Juan got through to the desk sergeant and word filtered out for the officers to simply do the intake. They collected handguns, but thanks to Juan, mine was returned to me before I was allowed to leave. The uniforms were professional, and seemed to handle the routine capably. But as the officers were finishing up, one of them informed us that while we were all being released, we would likely be called for follow-up questioning.

"Wait a minute," I said to the lead officer who appeared to be in charge. "You're not detaining Butterworth?"

"Sorry, no reason to. We have nothing firm to hold him on."

"Look, this guy has admitted to embezzling and more. We have a lot on him."

"Where's your evidence?

And therein was our problem. Miles' secret office was now fully locked, the janitors were long since gone, and we had no access to a DVD player. We certainly couldn't show them the laptop Sal pilfered from Isabelle's office because that would be far more problematic for Sal. A field officer is going to first be suspicious of a computer that may have been stolen, rather than the files that were contained in the ill-gotten item. And even if they were to look at the files, it was highly unlikely that an officer working the midnight shift would be able to understand the complexities of financial fraud. Especially while we were standing around in an industrial parking lot at three in the morning.

"I think you'd need to trust us," I said. "I spent 13 years on the job, if that will buy me any credibility. I worked out of the Broadway Precinct back then."

"Why'd you leave?" he asked.

I sighed. "Long story."

"Aren't they all," he smirked.

"Look, if you let this guy go," I said, "there's reason to believe he may come after Sal Valdez. This is now a situation where you may be putting someone's life in jeopardy."

"And I keep hearing about what a bad guy this Butterworth is, but he's got a license for that weapon.

Carrying it is something else. So we'll confiscate the gun for now. Best we can do."

"Would a call from Juan Saavedra help?

"Has Lt. Saavedra seen any of this evidence?"

"Not yet," I admitted.

"Then I don't think so."

And so no arrests were made and we were all allowed to leave. Despite my continued pleas to detain Butterworth, I couldn't provide them with any substantive proof on him yet; I needed to meet with Juan before we could move forward on anything. This shift of police officers were not going to be persuaded about anything tonight. Butterworth was going to be at-large, at least for another day, and we would simply have to deal with that. Sal was the one who was most at risk; the cane would only provide so much protection. Even owning a gun was no guarantee. I certainly didn't want him to meet the same fate as Henry Simon, the security guard up in Las Vegas. His death wasn't my fault, but it still weighed on my mind. Like most everything else these days.

"Sal," I said quietly, leading him away from the others, "I think it might be best if you didn't go home tonight."

His face tightened. "I can take care of myself, *señor*."

"I know you can. But there's a lot at stake here, and I'm sure Butterworth and his cronies can easily find out where you live."

"What are you suggesting?"

"I live in an apartment building with a security gate. My personal info is unlisted and I've made sure it's been scrubbed off the Internet. I'm not a homeowner, so there are no public records with my home address. Come and bunk with me for a couple of days in Santa Monica. I've got a pull-out sofa bed that's comfortable. You'll be safe and so will Isabelle's laptop."

Sal looked down at the ground for a minute as he weighed options in his mind. Other than his pride in being self-reliant, I didn't see any obstacle to my plan, nor a better one about to spring forward. Neither did he.

"Okay," he agreed.

I told Sal to follow me in his car. I offered Chase a place to stay as well, but he resolutely declined, saying he had a wife and kids to look after. I suggested to Chase that he call in sick rather than go to work the next day. To that, he gave no objection and said he could use a day off.

"There's one other thing," I said to Chase.

"What's that?"

"That gun you keep hidden under the driver's seat in the van?"

Chase stared at me. "How do you know about that?"

"I just do. Keep it on you for a few days."

Nodding solemnly, Chase agreed. He kept asking how I learned about the gun, but I just waved it off. "I'm pretty good at finding things," I said.

On the way home, I had a brief internal debate about calling Sal and stopping for an early breakfast at The Pantry again. Ultimately, I decided I needed sleep more than food right now. Tomorrow was going to be a mighty busy day.

Fourteen

It was a little past noon when I woke up, and my bedroom was awash in sunlight. Since the window faced west, the morning light filtered in delicately. No harsh glares or sun streaks crawling through to disturb me. Not that I normally slept in much past daybreak. The only times I allowed myself to doze well into the morning were those when Gail came over. And as I began to stir from my slumber today, I found myself missing her, even though it had been less than three days since our return from Vegas.

I got up and made a pot of French roast. I had slept for a long time and felt good. Last night was productive in many ways. When you have a breakthrough after a lot of hard work, that delicious feeling of satisfaction settles in. Whatever bumps and bruises and stresses I had to endure now seemed eminently worth it. Nothing is better than cracking a case. I just needed to put the finishing touches on this one.

Sal passed on coffee and said he was going to go for a long walk by the bluffs overlooking the ocean. "I don't get to the beach much these days," he said. "Might as well enjoy it while I can. Besides, I'm supposed to walk a few miles a day for the therapy on my hip."

I called Detective DeSanto and gave him a brief rundown on what transpired at Malco last night, after we had uncovered the evidence surrounding Miles' death. He agreed there wasn't much we could do about Butterworth in the short run. By now he could be halfway to Argentina.

I called Gail, and the simple sound of her sweet voice on the other end of the line made my heart sing. The little things in life can be as precious as a diamond.

"It's good to hear your voice," I said.

"Yours too, *compadre*. I didn't hear from you yesterday. I always worry a little."

"No need. I have everything under control."

Gail laughed. "My, oh my. I don't know where you get that confidence."

"It's the belief that today is going to be a better day than yesterday. And tomorrow will be better than today."

"That sounds like it came from a preacher."

"I think I stole it from a greeting card."

"For a moment there, I was wondering if I was talking to my boyfriend."

"I like the term boyfriend," I mused. "Sounds a lot more intimate than partner."

"You know the reality is the same."

"Yeah, it is."

"So how are you doing, honey? Staying out of trouble, I hope."

"Not really."

"Uh-oh."

"But the good news is I think we've cracked the Malco case wide open."

"You found proof of who's involved in the thefts?"

"Pretty close on that. And we also found out who killed Miles."

"Wow. You've had a productive week. I can't wait to hear about it."

"And I can't wait to hear about the job with the City Attorney. How about dinner tomorrow night? It'll kick off a great weekend."

"Works for me."

I showered and dressed and tried to move my thoughts back to my speech this afternoon at SC. I had a rough idea of what I wanted to say, but was struggling to find the right words. I knew that sometimes when I stood up and spoke in public, the words flowed out effortlessly. Other times they came out in a halting way that was as awkward for me as it was for the audience. I wasn't a naturally gifted speaker when it came to large gatherings. But although I didn't know most of USC's current players individually, I did know this type of group very well.

It was a warm day and I arrived on campus a little before 3:00. Entering the McKay Center, I wandered around for a few minutes before stopping by Coach Cleary's office. I said hello to Sean, who told me everyone was waiting for me in the team meeting room. As I started to walk out, he asked me to wait, and dug into his desk drawer. Pulling out a large envelope, he said it contained two field passes for Saturday's game, in addition to four tickets.

"Sorry about these tickets not being exactly on the 50-yard line. Coach said you'd understand."

"Sure," I laughed. "The UCLA game is always a hot ticket."

"Especially this year. The winner is one step away from the Rose Bowl. New Year's Day in Pasadena. It's big."

"Nothing like it," I said, and thanked him for his help. I had played in two Rose Bowl games myself and they held a very special place in my memories.

I needed a few minutes to find the auditorium. This was where the players and coaches gathered as a group. Typically, the coaches went over general plans about the upcoming game or disseminated news they wanted to share with the team as a whole. After that, they would break up and go off with their position coaches.

The auditorium was abuzz with conversation, and by my estimate it was filled with close to 100 players. The majority were African-American, but they were all between 18 and 23 and most appeared to be in incredible shape. The players often sat together by position. The linemen were the most noticeable, given that they were huge and often tipped the scales at over 300 pounds. But everyone else was very taut and solid and had arms the size of many people's legs. The biggest difference between now and when I played was that virtually every player was rippling with muscles. Even the kickers looked like they worked out vigorously. This was a group of extremely strong men, and they exuded the indefatigable confidence of youth and infallibility.

Johnny Cleary nodded to me, and I moved to the front of the auditorium. A number of assistant coaches came over and shook hands with me. Johnny motioned me aside and told me he was going to take care of some team business and then introduce me. After a few minutes of housekeeping items, Johnny began to give an introduction.

"Guys, we have a special guest today. Most of you won't recognize his name, but he is one of the Trojan players who helped make this university great. He never got his shot in the NFL because of a freak injury that happened off the field. But when he played here he was the heart and soul of the team. I know that because we played in the same secondary. You know I played cornerback here at SC about a million years ago. This man's name is Burnside and he played behind me at free safety. I want you all to stand up and give him a big Trojan welcome."

And with that, the players in the room rose in unison and began applauding and cheering. I was taken aback at first. I was expecting a polite round of applause, but the noise was deafening as players cheered and whooped. I smiled, waved, and motioned for them to sit down.

"Thank you. That's really nice of you, I appreciate it, I really do. Especially since none of you guys know who the hell I am."

The room roared with laughter. I began to get a good feeling about this.

"I'm going to talk to you like the grown men you are. I know some of you are still teenagers or in your early 20s, but you're men. And I've seen the effort you've put in this year. You're 10-1 and ranked in the top five in the country. You're among the most talented group of players USC has ever put together. But on Saturday against UCLA, that isn't going to mean so much.

"We all know about this rivalry. A lot of you grew up in So Cal and have been playing with or against these guys since Pop Warner. You're good, they're good. Let me tell you how you're going to look back on this game one day. I can sum it all up in one word. Effort.

"Everything comes down to effort. And you get to decide on just how much effort. How much effort you're going to put in. It's not just about *X*'s and *O*'s. It's about trying. It's about giving your all. And no one can make that decision but you. You decide just how hard you're going to try. You decide how much effort you exert. You decide how much of *you* is going to be in this game. You decide how you'll look back on this game one day.

"Some of you have heard the name Vince Lombardi. And you know Vince Lombardi was one of the greatest football coaches ever. He was once quoted as saying, 'Winning isn't everything, it's the only thing.' And you know what? He later said he regretted putting it in that way. What he meant to say was that winning isn't everything, what's important is doing everything you can, to put your team in a position to win. It's about focus, it's about hard work, it's about dedication. It's about you giving it every last ounce of energy you've got.

"There are going to be days when the football just doesn't bounce your way. No one wins every single game they play. But the guys who succeed in this sport - and in life - give it their best all the time. They don't hold back. And it's hard to think that one day you're going to be old like me. Or Coach Cleary over there," I said, jerking my thumb towards him. "But you will be. It happens to everyone. And the last thing you ever want to think is, oh, I wish I had tried harder when I was younger. I wish I had done the work. I wish I had given it everything.

"You've heard the saying, 'Leave it all on the field.' That means putting every fiber of your being into performing at as high a level as you possibly can. This means doing the things that other guys aren't doing. This is what makes you different. What makes you stand out. What makes you get on the field more. What allows you to make plays. What makes the coaches notice you. What makes the NFL notice you.

"Let me tell you something. I wasn't the fastest guy on my team, I wasn't the strongest guy, the biggest guy, the smartest guy. Well... maybe I *was* the smartest," I smiled. Laughter filled the room.

"But I worked *hard*. Really hard. I tried to work harder than anyone else. I was one of the first guys on the practice field every day, and one of the last to leave. I pressed my coaches about what I needed to do to get better. I studied a lot of film to see where I could improve. But what I really did was focus on doing what I needed to do to raise my game to the highest level.

"How many of you do this? How many of you can honestly say you give it your all on every play? I know how tired you get, how much energy it takes. I'm not saying it's easy. But what I am saying is this. If you want to succeed, you have to work for it. And work really hard. People don't realize what you have to give up to become great. What you have to promise to yourself to become great. And live up to it. This has to be your creed. Your belief. What you do every single day.

"You know, we only get one thing in life. And we all get the same thing. We get time on this earth. And we don't know how much time we have. Which is why we can't waste any. Time slows down for no one. It's all we have. And it's not as much as you may think. It goes by fast.

"I had a shot at the NFL. But I busted up my knee and

back then they didn't have the medical advances we have today. But working hard led me somewhere else, into a career in law enforcement. Now I have my own agency. My work is interesting. It's fascinating. It's challenging. I meet all sorts of people. Most of them I can help." I stole a glance at Marcellus. He was staring at me unblinking, his mouth slightly agape. "But I can help people because I work really hard at it. And the reward isn't always in money."

"If the numbers are correct, maybe seven or eight of you will be drafted into the NFL each year. A few more will catch on as free agents. Some of you will go on to make it in the league for a while. And when you're on that 53-man roster, you know you'll be making a lot of money. More money than you can make doing practically anything else at your age. But the average tenure in the NFL is three years. Three. Years. I think back to the guys from USC who were drafted ten years ago. I think only a couple of them are still playing. And not all the others are doing so well.

"This sport is brutal. And not just physically. You make a high profile mistake, whether on the field or off, and you may be gone for good. There aren't a lot of second chances in the NFL. If you're lucky you'll get one, maybe two shots. And that's why you need to prepare for life after football.

"Some of you love the game and will wind up as coaches. Some of you will move into other careers. But no matter what career you have, no matter what job you do, no matter what endeavor you're involved in. The harder you work at things, the more you will put yourself in a position to be successful. There is just no substitute for hard work. No substitute for effort.

"Try and think about just what it is you really want. And then put everything into getting it. You may need to make a course correction at some point. The very few who play in the NFL for a long time and invest well, they can retire and play golf the rest of their lives. But for the other 99 percent of us, we'll have to work at something. And the only way to do it successfully is by exerting that *effort*."

I paused and looked around. No one was daydreaming. No one's eyes were glazed over. No one was checking their watch. No one was leaning back in their chair. I think my talk was resonating. So I decided to lighten the mood.

"There's a story I want to share with you. It's about a great player who tried hard almost all the time. But he let his guard down for one moment. It was back during my sophomore year, and it happened in the UCLA game. They were up by 3 points, and there was about 20 seconds to go in the first half. UCLA had the ball down on our 5-yard line. The QB dropped back a step and then threw a quick bubble screen. They had been throwing that little pass the whole game, must have completed it half a dozen times. It usually only went for 5 or 10 yards, but those yards add up. The cornerback they were targeting was a guy named Johnny Cleary. I, uh, think you know him."

I looked over at Johnny and he was looking at the floor, shuffling his feet, trying to hold a smile back. He knew what was coming.

"But Coach Cleary, he read the play the whole way. They put a couple of blockers out there, but they never had a chance. Johnny stepped in front of the receiver and picked it off. And he had clear daylight ahead of him. He ran 90 yards and he was on his way to the end zone. And he was quick. No one was quicker than Johnny Cleary back then.

"But you know, they say the fastest guy on the football field is a quarterback who just had a pass intercepted. And that Bruin quarterback ran the length of the field and not only tackled Johnny before he got to the end zone, but he stripped the ball from him. That's right. Coach relaxed for that split second when he got near that goal line. And you know what happened next?"

I looked out at the team, and there was now a lot of grinning and laughing. Some guys were clapping their hands. You don't often get to see your head coach a little red-faced. Except maybe after a bucket of Gatorade is dumped on him during a post-game celebration.

"Well, there was one guy who didn't stop for a second. One guy who had a perfect view of what was happening. Because I was trailing Johnny on the play. I wanted to be the first one to jump on him and celebrate. I wanted to share his success. Our success. But the next thing you know, that football is rolling on the ground. And because I was running hard behind Johnny, I was right there. I scooped up the ball and ran five yards into the end zone. So Coach does all the work, he reads the play, he gets the pick, he runs 90 yards with the rock. But I'm the one who gets to score the touchdown."

The players were hooting with laughter. And above the din, I heard the voice of Marcellus Williams call out, "Hey Coach! Is that why we never run the bubble screen here? That's a play we should run on Saturday! They'll never see it coming!"

Johnny held up his hands. "Look, that's not the reason we haven't run bubble screens. It's a high-risk play. Like we just heard." He turned to me and smiled an evil smile.

"Burnside makes a great point. You have to play hard on every play. Most of us are guilty of relaxing once in a while. But what he says makes all the sense in the world. You never know when an opportunity presents itself. You have to be prepared. And being prepared means working hard. And putting in that 100 percent effort all the time. On every play. We only get one shot a year at UCLA and this is it. This is the big game. There is nothing like it in college football, a cross-town rivalry between two nationally ranked schools. We need to make every play count and we need total effort throughout the whole game.

"I'd like to thank Burnside for coming by and talking to us today. He's going to lead us on the field Saturday. Everyone needs to think about what he just said and take it to heart. We're going to work hard, we're going in totally prepared and we're going to win this thing."

With that, Johnny dismissed the team and the players began to disperse. A number came over and shook my hand and told me how much they appreciated my talk. A few said they thought my words were really important to them. And when most of the players had left the room, Marcellus Williams quietly approached me.

"That speech was amazing," he said.

"Thank you. This is the first time I've had the honor of addressing the team. I'm glad it went over well."

Marcellus drew in a breath. "I heard from Roper," he said.

"And?"

"Man, you really got through to him."

"Good."

"Yeah, you got through real good. He told me not to worry, he's not going to make trouble. He wants to stay in touch 'cause when I go pro in a couple of years, he says he can get some deals for me. Knows the guys at Nike, some record labels, too. He says he wants to help me, not mess me up."

I shrugged. "Maybe he can. You'll have to make that decision. But you'll be in a better place to do so in a couple of years. You'll know more, about him, about yourself, about the world you're in. I'm glad he agreed to back off. No one should put an 18-year-old college freshman in that position."

"Mmm-hmmm," he said. "So you made this go away. I don't know how you did it or what you did. But it changed everything. And I wanted to thank you, man. Thank you very much."

We shook hands and I made sure to squeeze tightly, lest I get overcome by one of the strongest, most massive hands I had ever touched. I wished him good luck in the game on Saturday. He smiled and said hard work would get him farther than luck. I smiled back. Sometimes the message gets through.

*

The drive down to the Broadway Precinct would normally only take 10 minutes in clear traffic. But in rush hour, 10 minutes equates to 45 minutes. After slogging through the stop-and-go on the Harbor Freeway, I finally exited and found parking near the police station.

Both Juan Saavedra and Roberto DeSanto were waiting for me and quickly ushered me into a 1980s style A/V room. I set the DVD into the tray and it took about 30 seconds to get going. The images finally flashed on the TV screen. The lighting wasn't ideal and the audio left something to be desired. But there was no doubt about who was who. We watched quietly and then Juan asked to see it again. And again for a third time. And then a fourth. I was tempted to ask if the additional viewings revealed anything new, but decided my acerbic wit would be out of place here.

"I think we have enough to swear out a warrant," Roberto said.

"Tough to argue with something that's in living color," Juan added. "So how did you get a hold of this?"

"The security badge Miles arranged for me. It gave me access to the building. Apparently that did not include Miles' office. One of the janitors let me in."

"And this DVD was just lying around?" Juan said, looking at me.

"No. Miles had a special room set up for surveillance so he could watch people around the company. I guess he was pretty paranoid."

"Sure sounds like."

"Anyway, Miles had placed a hidden camera in his office. No one knew about it."

"Except you. How'd that happen?"

"One of the installers helped. Chase Walker, you guys talked to him, beefy little guy with the big moustache," I reminded them. "Look, I'd appreciate it if you could minimize his involvement here. He helped me but he wants to keep a low profile. He'll answer your questions but he's got a record and wants to go through this as anonymously as he can."

"I'll see what I can do."

"You won't have a problem getting a confession once you show this. Be better for them to cop a plea and get life. They're looking at lethal injection otherwise."

Juan sat back and looked at me. "This is good work," he finally said. "Whatever way you got it. And yeah, we'll probably get them to plea. Biggest problem we have is how we find this person."

"I have an idea."

"Geez, why am I surprised at that."

"Just a hunch. If I'm correct, I'll call you right away. Should be this evening. But this is a little outside the jurisdiction of the LAPD."

"Oh, you're going to make the collar yourself, are you?"

"Look, if this person smells police in the area, they are going to disappear. For good. I can get to them. They won't suspect me. I know what I'm doing."

"Sometimes that's part of the problem," Juan said.

"There won't be any problems," I said, and then remembered something. I reached into my back pocket. "Here's four tickets to Saturday's game. Just like you asked for."

DeSanto frowned as Juan accepted the tickets and put them away. "Let me guess," he said, "that comes with a favor attached."

"All part of doing business in this town, Roberto," Juan smiled at him. "Don't worry. Burnside's gonna take care of you one day."

I rolled my eyes. "Thanks, Lieutenant."

"Don't mention it."

"Yeah," I said. "So, we're picking up Billy the Fixer tomorrow afternoon."

"Where?"

"Just off of Robertson. Near Beverly Hills." I wrote down the address and handed it to him.

"Give me a call when you're there," Juan said. "I'll arrange for a couple of uniforms to pick him up. And hey Burnside. Thanks for the tickets."

"Maybe I'll see you there."

Juan looked down and carefully inspected them. "Nice. These look like 30-yard line. I can live with that. Where are your seats?"

I smiled. "You'll see."

*

Leaving the Broadway Precinct, I drove a little ways down the crowded Harbor Freeway before heading west. It was a nice warm day that was becoming a nice, warm evening. It was the type of evening that was perfect for being in Manhattan Beach. But for one person in particular, that would not be the case.

Manhattan Beach was a small city that managed to be both ritzy and laid back. Surfers and sophisticates. It was a community where brand new multimillion dollar architectural masterpieces dotted the strand overlooking the beach. And right behind them were often small, nondescript bungalows that were built 60 years earlier, and had not been updated since.

I drove all the way down 16th Street until it ended, and pulled into a driveway a few yards from the Strand. There were a number of beautiful homes on the block, and this was one of them. I walked past a very small, grassy area and onto the beach facing property. I rang the bell and a minute later Clara Larson answered the door.

"Burnside. This is a surprise."

"Sorry I didn't call first."

"No, no, it's all right," she said, opening the door and inviting me in.

"Actually, I'm here to see Eddie. Is he around?"

"Why yes. Wait one moment."

I cooled my heels in the foyer as I waited for a few minutes. The floor was a polished gold tile, and a crystal chandelier hung from the ceiling. The far wall facing the ocean had floor-to-ceiling windows that displayed a beautiful orange sunset, framed by the dark blue water and a light blue sky. Finally Eddie Larson appeared. He walked over to me, and a bit of a limp was evident.

"Hi there," he said. "Surprised to see you here."

"Hope it's not a bad time," I said and pointed to the ground. "Is your foot okay?"

Eddie shrugged. "Yeah, must have twisted it playing volleyball or something, it's a little swollen. No biggie. Want a beer?"

I shook my head no. "Actually, I was hoping to have a

word with you. Care to take a walk on the Strand?"

"Okay," he said. "I'll be back in a little while, Mom."

"Is everything all right, Burnside?" asked Clara.

"Yes," I said. "I'll give you an update, maybe tomorrow. Will you be home?"

"I'm sure I will. I have nowhere else to go these days."

Eddie was wearing long, bronze colored shorts and a dark blue t-shirt with a zipped light jacket. He slipped on a pair of wraparound Maui Jim sunglasses. We walked a block or so and talked about nothing in particular. Just how beautiful the sunset was, and how much Manhattan Beach reminded him of Hawaii. I noticed a bulge above Eddie's left hip and knew he was ready for trouble. And trouble was what I was bringing.

"It's over, Eddie." I said as we kept walking.

"What's over?"

"You know what I'm talking about. It took a while but we finally learned what happened. Why it happened is another story. But that isn't our concern now."

Eddie drank all this in and kept walking. "You think so, huh?"

I walked evenly with him, keeping the same pace. "Your Dad left us a trail of breadcrumbs. He had his office wired and the whole scene was videotaped. The camera got a clear shot of you. Not that that was imperative, your voice was enough. We know you shot your father to death. We have the proof. There's no doubt."

Eddie stopped suddenly. "How much do you want?" he demanded.

I shook my head. "I'm not for sale."

"Everyone's for sale."

"Not me."

"Everyone has their price."

"I don't. At least not in money. It's over."

Eddie stepped back away from me. He was a hardened criminal, a cold-blooded killer, but his actions were predictable. As predictable as a quarterback telegraphing a pass to the defense by eyeing only one receiver. He reached for the weapon, but I had my gun drawn by then. Holding it in my right hand, I grabbed Eddie's left arm and jerked it away from his body, twisting the arm hard behind his back in the process.

"We can do this the easy way or the hard way," I hissed.

Eddie didn't answer, but his rapid breathing told me not to mess around. I cut his left foot out from under him, tripping him and driving my left knee into his lower back. He landed face-first onto the pavement. Removing a pair of plastic flex cuffs, I wrapped his wrists tightly together. I yanked his pistol out of its holster and stuffed it into my belt. Lifting him to his feet, we walked over to the side of a nearby house. I led him into an alley and sat him down against a wall. Taking out my phone, I glanced up at the address on the house, and called Juan Saavedra. After telling him where we were, I noticed a couple of passersby staring at us. They looked to be in their early 20s, and were wearing black wet suits. Their light blond hair was long and wet and tangled from being in the ocean.

"Hey, what's happening over here?" one of them asked, and they stepped towards us.

I raised a hand and instructed them to stop. "Police

business," I said in a loud voice. "Come any closer and you'll be arrested and booked."

They looked at each other, shrugged, and kept walking. I sat down across from Eddie, close enough to talk, far away enough so that he wouldn't try kicking me to get one last chance for freedom. Something he might never taste again.

"You know I've got the best lawyers," he said. "I don't care what's on the video. They'll get me off. There's always a technicality."

I shook my head. "I've been in law enforcement for quite a while. It's over Eddie. And it's not just you that's involved here. Even if this case wasn't air-tight, your partner isn't as tough as you are. They'll crack."

His breathing seemed to stop for a moment. It was as if the reality of the situation had just kicked in. He stared ahead blankly. He was looking at me, but it didn't seem as if he was really focused on anything. I knew I only had a few minutes.

"So tell me something, Eddie. You know you did it and I know you did it. What I don't know is why."

He shook his head. "It's all about money," he said. "That's why I do things. That's why everyone does things."

"But your father, Eddie? You'd kill your own father?"

Eddie looked off at the ocean. The surf was calm today, and the waves that were forming were mild. The water was as smooth as glass in the distance. A warm breeze had started to blow.

"My Dad was a prick," he began. "A real son-of-a-bitch. He didn't give a rat's ass about his kids. He loved the business. And the university of course. That really gnawed at him, when I didn't go to SC. He felt like he had failed somehow. He just didn't understand I didn't give a damn about that stuff. I told him not everyone had to be like their old man."

"You didn't want to go into the family business. That must have bugged him. What was this stuff about working on Wall Street?"

"I needed to give him a story to tell people. It's not like he could up and tell his cronies what his son did for a living."

"Not your typical career choice," I said.

"No, but like I told you. It's all about money. Dad wouldn't pay for college unless it was SC. I told him I got a scholarship, but that was bogus. I fell in with some people who showed me I could make some big money taking people out. Some *really* big money."

"Wouldn't your Dad bring you into his business at Malco?"

Eddie shook his head no. "This was going to be Peter's company when Dad stepped down. But Dad wasn't stepping down. The business was his life."

"And then the business started to tank."

Eddie froze. "You know about that?"

"I know Malco was in serious financial trouble. They're already in debt. From what I understand, the business probably wouldn't have lasted more than a couple more years. Then everything would be gone."

He nodded slowly. "You really dug into this."

"Someone was ripping the company off. That's why I was brought in."

"Malco is done. It's just a matter of time. Dad built the

company, but he was going to go down in flames. If Dad stayed in charge, I'd have wound up with nothing. The business would be gone."

"And that bit up in Vegas with the security guard. That was your handiwork, also?"

Eddie shook his head no. "Believe it or not, I had nothing to do with that guard. I was up in Vegas on another matter. You know. Trying to sign Megawatt. Somehow you got your nose into that situation, too."

"Everything stemmed from what Miles was doing," I said. "And your Dad knew the state of the Company. He was introducing football players to agents. Partly because he knew he'd get a cut if they signed with them. He was looking out for himself."

"Yeah. I'm the one who introduced Dad to Roper. I've worked with Roper for years. We go way back."

"You have your fingers in a lot of pies," I said. "In this case, it started with Miles, but all roads led to Eddie Larson here."

"I'm just looking to get by. To get what I could, while I could. To get what's mine. You know I stand to inherit one-third of Malco. But one-third of nothing is nothing."

Some things were starting to fall into place. There seemed to be multiple conspiracies being played out here, and they all overlapped. "So once I started investigating, you got nervous."

"We could handle the police. They're outsiders and they have lots of other things on their plates. The way I set things up, the only way someone could have unraveled this is from the inside. That's why you were such a concern. I needed to get you away from the investigation into what happened to Dad."

"And your Mom? Were you going to knock her off, too?"

Eddie gave me a weird look. "C'mon bro," he said incredulously. "She's my mother."

Now it was my turn to look out at the waves. I had no idea what made this family tick, or why human life was considered expendable just so certain people could grab more money. Their whole story was sounding more and more like a Greek tragedy.

In the distance I heard a siren, and it grew closer until it became a loud wail I could feel in my gut. I saw one of the surfers again, standing on the strand, this time pointing at us. A pair of brown uniformed officers hustled into the alley.

"What's going on here?" one of the uniforms demanded.

"Citizen's arrest," I said. "This man is wanted for murder."

"In whose jurisdiction?"

I blinked a couple of times. "LAPD. Chief of detectives at the Broadway Precinct is Lt. Juan Saavedra. He'll be here soon."

"Uh-huh. Why don't you two get up. Keep your hands where we can see them."

A few minutes passed, but Juan finally arrived and began debriefing the uniforms. A pair of LAPD cruisers arrived shortly thereafter, and after a lengthy discussion, Eddie Larson was taken into custody. He didn't bother to say goodbye. And I never got my plastic flex cuffs back.

Fifteen

The next morning brought a continuation of the warm weather, although the forecast predicted rain in a few days. A few clouds were forming in the distance. Fortunately it would likely come after the USC-UCLA game. The last thing I wanted to do was stand on the sidelines with Gail in a steady downpour.

I received a call from Amanda Hertz, and we had clear access to the house later that afternoon. I confirmed the time and location with Billy and then talked to Juan. I also called Gail to let her know my plans for the day and to talk about dinner that night.

"Amanda," Gail mused. "Have you figured out what else is going on with her?"

"No, not yet. I guess I'll find out later. Are you still interested in meeting a true sociopath today?"

"Billy the Fixer? Sure. I don't want to miss an opportunity like that."

"The whole process will probably take 15 minutes," I estimated. "We'll meet him and then the police will come by and take him away. Simple and routine."

"I like seeing you work," she said. "And after meeting Amanda, I'm curious what else Billy stole from her."

I was also wondering what else Billy had stolen. "Okay. I can't imagine there'll be anything that comes close to what happened up in Vegas."

"What happened in Vegas, honey," she said, practically smiling into the phone, "stays in Vegas."

Hanging up, I walked into the living room and saw that Sal had Isabelle's laptop open, and was combing through it further. I had made an appointment for Sal and I to meet with Mark Lutz in the Financial Crimes Division. I knew that proving embezzlement was going to be a lot harder than wrapping up a murder case.

"There's just so much here," he said, as we packed up and prepared to leave. We rode the elevator downstairs into my garage. Opening the Pathfinder, he placed the laptop and his Bad Ass cane carefully on the floor. I pointed to the cane. "Given that we're headed to the Parker Center, I doubt you'll need that for protection."

Sal smiled. "I also use it for support. My hip may take a while to fully heal."

"Have you spoken to anyone at Malco since the other night?"

"Yes. I haven't said anything about what happened, but I guess one of the security guards told people about the police being there. They think there was a break-in or something at headquarters. The place is abuzz with rumors. I gather no one has heard from Butterworth. No surprise, he hasn't shown up at work. Neither has Isabelle."

"No surprise at all," I agreed.

"I'm so sorry the police let Butterworth get away."

"True. But as the saying goes, he can run but he can't hide."

We drove downtown, found a space on the street, and entered the Parker Center. Emptying our pockets at the entrance, we walked through the metal detectors and gathered up our things again. It took a few minutes to find the Financial Crimes Division.

Mark Lutz was in his late 40s, with black and gray hair and a black and gray moustache. We found him on the phone, but he motioned for us to sit in the chairs opposite his desk. He finished his conversation after a few minutes.

"Gentlemen," he said, getting up and shaking hands. "Nice to meet you."

"Likewise," I said. "We have the sting set up for Billy Ray Fox later today. Juan said he'd help bring him in. I have a client who'll press charges. She's pretty ticked off."

Mark Lutz nodded. "Okay. I've got half a dozen more victims who say they'll testify. This guy'll go away for a while. No doubt."

"Great."

"But you said you had something else."

I turned to Valdez. "Sal, you want to take the lead here?"

Valdez began showing Mark a potpourri of doctored financial statements, forged checks and email communications that linked Isabelle Larson, Glen Butterworth and Adam Barber to everything from fraud and conspiracy to outright grand theft. Mark Lutz maintained little expression on his face as he listened and processed things. He waited until Sal was finished before he spoke again.

"What you've put together is impressive. But it's all been gathered illegally. You've taken company-owned property. Not to say a case can't be built here. There's an obvious amount of large scale criminal activity. But you're also talking about a privately held company. And one of the principal ringleaders is the daughter of the CEO. Well, former CEO to be accurate. And I'm not sure what her equity position is within the company. I know it's unlikely, but she could practically argue she's stealing her own money. The issue will be who is filing the complaint here?"

"Isn't this a corporation?" Sal asked.

"Yes it is, but I gather it's wholly owned by the Larson family."

"And because this is essentially a family business, we have to involve a family member?"

"Yes and given the circumstances that arose over the past day or two, there may be a lot of difficulty in doing that," Lutz said, wryly.

Valdez looked a little crestfallen. "This seems so wrong."

"It's not a lost cause," Lutz continued. "This is something the IRS would be very interested in. And there could be some RICO implications too. But moving a lot of these charges forward is going to require cooperation and support from a family member. It isn't as simple as just getting a warrant."

"Not going to be such an easy thing to get a family member to press charges against another member of the Larson clan," I said.

"Not easy," Lutz repeated, "but this is obviously one strange family."

We thanked Lutz and walked out of his office and out of the building. Neither myself nor Valdez spoke until we climbed into the Pathfinder.

"I am so disappointed," he said blankly. "It feels like justice is hard to come by. I can't imagine Mrs. Larson or

Peter believing any of this about Isabelle."

"We'll see. Clara's got a lot to deal with right now. Her whole world has come crashing down."

"Yes," he said. "Mrs. Larson has been dealt a rotten hand."

Sal had no idea just how rotten that was. And while I wasn't sure having a union leader in the room would be helpful here, Sal had played a critical role in our getting us to where we were now. I needed to show Clara what had happened, and maybe now was the time for everything to be placed on the table.

"I guess we go see her," I finally said.

"I guess we do."

*

On the drive to Manhattan Beach, I tried to piece everything together in a way that was logical and explainable and made sense. But nothing about this situation was logical or explainable or made any sense. This case was stitched together through a series of despicable acts by despicable people. I suspected there would be no happy endings for anyone involved.

I parked the Pathfinder in the same space I found the other night. The morning air was a little damp by the beach, but the sun was coming out, breaking through the marine layer. We knocked on the front door and Clara Larson opened it. She did not look well.

Clara appeared disheveled and her eyes were red. She was dressed in a maroon jogging outfit and her white helmet of hair was unkempt. Her face was lined with pain, her eyes were cloudy and unfocused, and her movements unsteady. She invited me in, but as I moved inside I had to grab her arm to keep her from tripping and falling onto the gold tile floor. I led her to a thick, tawny colored sofa in the living room and sat down next to her. I searched for words I could say. None came quickly. But I had to start somewhere. After a few long minutes, I spoke.

"I'm sorry Clara," I said in a low, sympathetic voice. "I'm so sorry."

She nodded absently and paused for a moment to catch her breath and focus her thoughts. I looked around the room at the plush surroundings. In addition to a variety of USC memorabilia, a series of brightly colored African masks were hung along the far wall.

"I feel as if I'm caught in a bad dream," she said. "A week ago, we had a minor problem with theft at the company. Today my life has become a complete catastrophe."

"I cannot even imagine what you're going through. Again, I'm very sorry."

"It's not your fault, Burnside. I just don't understand any of it."

"I'm not sure anyone fully does."

"How could Eddie have done this? Is it really true? And everything else? As a mother I find all of this to be insane. It makes no sense."

"I can understand why it's hard to believe."

"The police say you provided them with documented proof. But they didn't go any further. Just what is this proof you have?"

"I'll show it to you," I said, and removed a copy of the DVD from my pocket. "It's gritty. I have to tell you that before you see it. You need to be prepared. And I want to give you the option of not seeing it. It has to be your choice."

"Oh I want to see it," she said. "It's better to know than to not know. I'm not going to live in a world of darkness. I want the truth, unvarnished as it might be. I have to know what happened to my family."

"Understood. And if you're up for it, Sal has some things he wants to show you."

I walked over to the Larsons' elaborate entertainment center to slip the DVD into the tray. I then turned on what had to be an 80 inch 4K TV that was mounted on the wall facing the sofa. A minute later an image appeared on the screen. It was a little grainy, but there was no question about who was who. The sound was very clear.

On the screen we saw two figures enter the office and sit down on the couch. From what Juan had told me, Miles had greeted Eddie at the front entrance on Saturday morning and ushered him into the building. We were able to make out the audio of the father-and-son exchange.

"How long's it been since you came by the old office?" Miles asked.

"A long time, Dad. Too long."

"I always dreamed the three of you kids would take over for me one day."

Eddie gave a laugh. "You've got Peter and Isabelle. That should be enough. More than enough, actually."

"Yeah, but we can always use another good mind working the business. That stinking Eagle Cable group. They just keep pecking away at us."

"What are they doing now?"

"They're dinging us for everything. They're doing surveys of customers and these bastards fine us if we get low scores. Even to the point of not paying us at all. They're a pack of damn criminals, they are. They just want to keep us from our money."

"Almost as bad as the IRS, Dad?" Eddie smiled, seemingly knowing the response.

"Oh, hell. Nothing is as bad as the IRS!" Miles crowed.

"How much trouble is the business in, Dad?"

"Eh. Look Eddie, it's not good but we'll weather the storm. Every few years the cable companies merge, and it takes the bloodsuckers a few years to pull their heads out of their asses and make a run at us. That's the window when we start making a lot of money again."

"Well until then at least you're getting some cash from Roper."

"Yeah, that's gravy. Easy for me to introduce players to him. If a guy hits it really big we all laugh our way to the bank. Those endorsement deals are unbelievably lucrative. And that Megawatt kid is a can't miss. Don't let that beast get away. Get him signed, sealed and delivered as soon as possible."

"I'm on it Dad. He's money. I'm reeling him in. Don't need to worry about that one."

"Eh, that's good. I don't know how you met up with that Roper fella but it's a lucky thing for us."

"I've helped him out of some jams."

"You know, you never really talk much about what you do. I know you work with some of those big shots on Wall Street now and then. Of course without a college degree I'm surprised they'd hire you as a consultant."

"I'm a specialist. I do things others can't do. Or won't do."

"Eh, well I'm glad you found your niche. I'm actually impressed you've been able to strike out on your own and be successful."

"You don't think Peter or Isabelle could do that?"

"Maybe. I don't know. Isabelle makes some poor decisions. Like having a fling with that operations chief we hired. That Butterworth. Always struck me as a bit of a huckster. Part of why I hired a private dick recently. We have a lot of product missing. I know that Valdez guy is out to get us. I just can't pin it on him. Those Spanish guys are pretty slippery, too"

Eddie stared at him. "And Peter?"

"I don't know. I wonder if Peter really has the stones to make it on his own. If I wasn't around, I get the feeling things would be even shakier than they are right now."

"You know that's the reason I'm here this morning, Dad."

"Eh, how's that? You told me you'd be in early."

"Yeah. I couldn't have anyone around to see this."

"See what?"

In what seemed like an effortless motion, Eddie Larson had a pistol in his right hand and aimed it at Miles. Stunned into silence for a second, Miles' mouth was open but no words came out. Slowly he began to rise from his chair.

"Now look here Eddie, I don't know what this is about."

"I think you do, Dad. It's about you."

"I'm your father for crissakes! What are you doing?"

"Father? You've been a lousy father from the day I was born. Everything was either your way or the highway. I chose the highway. But that's not why I'm going to do this. Not at all."

"Then why?! What are you doing this for?!"

"It's business, Dad. It's like you taught us. A long time ago. Everything comes down to money. Dollars and cents. Everything we do."

"Well, uh, yes ... but how the hell does that have anything to do with your pulling a gun on me? Your own father!"

"Because," Eddie said slowly, as if he were speaking to someone very slow."I'm being paid a lot of money here. It's like this, Dad. Peter wants to run things now at Malco."

And with that, a loud pop was audible. Then another pop, and then another as Eddie lowered the gun and continued firing until Miles fell helplessly to the floor. Placing the gun back into his jacket pocket, Eddie surveyed the room for a long moment. At one point he looked directly into the camera, fixating on what he likely thought was only a commemorative football helmet. He was obviously unaware that the camera in the helmet was recording every move he made.

Eddie left the office and the video stopped. I reached over for the remote and turned the TV off. Clara Larson sat very still next to me, and while she wasn't moving, a long, steady stream of tears were sliding down her face. Sal Valdez sat motionless on the couch. We continued to sit in silence for a few long minutes before I spoke again.

"I'm sorry I had to show you that. I can't even imagine what you're going through."

Clara struggled to find her voice. "I had to see it. I wouldn't have believed it if I hadn't seen it with my own two eyes. That explains some things. I haven't heard from Peter since you had Eddie arrested."

"Peter's been arrested, too," I told her, but I wondered if she even heard me.

"And I haven't heard anything from Isabelle, either," she said.

Valdez spoke. "Neither Isabelle nor Glen Butterworth showed up for work the past two days. My guess is the two of them have disappeared together. You may not hear from her again."

"But why?"

"She and Glen were behind the theft of the set-top boxes," Sal continued. "That guy they sent up to Vegas, Adam Barber, he was also part of the ring. Isabelle thought the company was going under soon, so I guess the three of them figured they'd get their share now while they could."

Clara looked at me. "Isabelle wasn't part of the scheme to shoot Miles?"

"No," I said. "Not from what I can tell. And that's what made this investigation so difficult to unravel. There were two conspiracies being played out simultaneously. Peter and Eddie were plotting to kill Miles, so Peter could take over the business. Isabelle was looting the company because she didn't think there would be much left once the cable vultures were done with them. She had more knowledge of the finances. All Peter saw was an opportunity to be king. And Eddie, well, you just saw how he makes his living."

"No matter that it was his own father."

"Didn't seem to faze him," I said.

"And Peter paid Eddie to do this horrible deed."

"Yes."

"And Isabelle would steal from her own family."

"She had some help, but yes."

Clara choked for a moment. "One week ago I had a husband running a business and three children with careers," she managed. "Today my husband is dead, my two sons are in jail and my daughter has disappeared. I suppose I still have a business, but not much of one apparently."

"Again, I'm sorry. But even a week ago, what you had wasn't what it seemed to be. You weren't seeing the whole picture. It's not your fault. You were screened from what was really happening."

"Oh but it was my fault, Burnside, it was. I didn't pay attention to what was happening. I didn't step in when Eddie left years ago. I could have insisted Miles help him. I could have been more involved in the business, understood more. It is absolutely my fault. But Mr. Valdez, you have something more?"

Sal spread out the documents on the coffee table and spent the next half-hour taking Clara through the levels of financial schemes and machinations that had plagued Malco. He turned on Isabelle's laptop and opened up countless pages, documenting how they had transferred money to off-shore accounts, developed a relationship with a Swiss bank, and even arranged with someone for money laundering. It was a Halloween bag of embezzlement and theft. It was larcenous behavior that could have only been achieved by someone in whom Miles Larson had put his utmost faith and trust. And while Peter had arranged the murder and Eddie had committed the act, I had a funny feeling this financial scheme was the betrayal that Miles would find the most disturbing. It involved, of course, his money.

And oddly, the pain Clara had exhibited just a short while earlier had seemingly begun to dissipate. Instead of grief, her expression had been replaced by anger. She no longer displayed the helpless look of despair. Rather, a gritty, steel backbone started to emerge as she began to clarify how these events had shaped her world. Her brutal honesty was impressive and that was perhaps a start towards trying to make herself whole again. Her life would never ever be the same, but she seemed to be able to quickly accept the unpleasant things she had to do, and the difficult road she would have to go down. She would have to do it alone and it would be filled with agony. Losing your whole family in such a short period, even within a scenario that had taken years to play out, was tragic beyond imagination.

"They start out crawling on all fours," she said, her face riddled with intensity. "Then you help them to stand on their own two feet. But it wasn't supposed to end like this for my three children."

*

Sal told me he had a friend nearby in Hermosa Beach who he wanted to visit, and they would give him a ride to pick up his car the next day. I offered to let him stay with me longer, but he said he would need to get home eventually. With Butterworth seemingly gone underground, the risk to Sal was probably minimal. I thanked him for everything; he had taken some really big risks to uncover and protect the truth.

My drive home from Manhattan Beach was a sober one. I went up Vista del Mar, the coastal route that offered a gorgeous view of Santa Monica Bay, and wound my way through Dockweiler Beach and the Ballona Wetlands. This was the morning commute some people employed to get to the Westside and to avoid the slow moving freeway traffic. By now, rush hour was over and I had the road largely to myself. It made the drive easier, but the magnitude of what had happened, and the devastating impact on Clara, still weighed heavily on my mind.

I went to my office and did some paperwork, hoping to take my mind off of the Larson family for a little while. The Malco check had finally cleared, so I paid a few bills, including my office rent. I received another confirmation call from Amanda Hertz. We were all set for this afternoon's meeting with Billy the Fixer. I reviewed my files on Billy and thought about how this afternoon would go. But as hard as I tried to focus, the face of Miles Larson, moments before he died, kept haunting me. He broke into my thoughts and occupied my mind. Miles had raised a monstrous brood. Sophocles would have had a field day studying them.

I always thought I'd have a family. I kept telling myself that one day it would happen, although my window for doing so was narrowing. But would I even want a family after seeing this type of an ending? Being a parent struck me as a lifelong job, one that you took on and never gave up. I kept reminding myself that what happened to the Larson family was an aberration, an anomaly, a gross exception to the rule. And I decided that if I were to have a family one day, the emphasis would not be on money or on business or on careers or on getting whatever you can in any way you can. There was a better script to follow and a better way to raise children. I knew it. I just struggled to figure out why Miles Larson didn't know it. Maybe the strategy that Miles' father employed, throwing Miles out of the house at age 18, was not the best parenting model he could have used. If he only knew how things would end up.

Gail and I had a late lunch before driving over to the house that Amanda had secured for our meeting with Billy. It was on a quiet street lined with silver maple trees, and there was an 'In Escrow' sign in the front yard. We arrived a little before 4:00pm and Amanda was waiting by the front door.

The house had that hollow, vacuous feeling of a home that hadn't been lived in. There was no furniture, no clothing in the closets, no dog wagging its tail. It was barren and empty and would serve our purpose fine, as far as I could tell. I turned to Amanda.

"Okay, we're good here."

"Excellent," she said.

"Now you need to leave."

"What?"

"Leave. Get out. You can't be here," I told her.

"No, no. I need to see this happen."

"You can't. If Billy spots you, he'll figure out what's going on. He'll run and you'll never see him again."

"I'll hide in the closet. He'll never know."

"He'll see your car."

"I'll move it."

"We can't take that chance."

Amanda looked pleadingly at Gail, but just got a shrug in return. "He knows what he's doing," Gail said. "You need to listen to him."

"You'll call me when it's done?" she asked in a resigned voice.

"Yes."

Taking a deep breath, Amanda walked out the door and got into her black BMW and drove off. I sighed, relieved, and called Juan to give him an update. He said he'd send a cruiser over, but it might take a while in rush hour traffic. And he certainly didn't want the unit to engage the siren and alert Billy as to what was going down. After hemming and hawing for a moment, he said he might drop by too. We waited about 10 minutes before there was a loud knock on the front door.

I opened the door to find not one, but two men standing there. One was a lean man about my age, with long sandy hair, a thick, blond goatee, and tattoos running up and down his arms. The other man was short and stout and his head was shaved.

"Hey," the man with the goatee said. "I'm Billy."

We shook hands and I invited them in. I didn't anticipate Billy bringing along an associate, a man he called George. This might complicate things. I introduced them to Gail and watched Billy give her the once over. A couple of times.

"You're looking to get central air in this place," Billy said.

"Right," I answered. "We're getting a couple of bids now."

Billy looked around. "Nice house. Yeah you'll definitely want to get AC. People think because they're on the Westside it's cooler, but I'll tell you, summer days can get pretty toasty here."

"Uh yeah," I said. "We don't take title until escrow closes next week. We don't live in the area. Heck, I'm not even sure what this neighborhood is like. It's just near our work."

"Don't worry about it," he said reassuringly. "You probably have a lot on your mind, buying a new place and all."

"Oh yeah," I said. "I've been real busy lately."

Billy asked if he could take a look around, and he and George moved from room to room, Billy jotting notes down on a pad, George following him, looking bored. George wore loose-fitting jeans and I noticed what seemed like the end of a box cutter sticking out of his back pocket. They crawled up in the attic for a few minutes and then went outside to look at the back yard. When they came back inside, Billy was nodding his head.

"This should be no problem at all. In fact, I can get you a deal on an AC unit. You should also replace the furnace, it's not in great shape. I can throw that in for free."

"Free?" I asked, wide eyed. "You'd do that?"

"Sure, you seem like good people. And I can pull out the furnace that's there and take it away. I'll just give it to my church. There's always someone who needs it."

"That's very generous of you," I said, marveling at Billy's Robin Hood act.

"Hey I try to help. You're both Christians, right?"

Gail and I looked at each other and then back at Billy. "Sure."

"I knew it," he said, nodding his head and spending too much of his time on Gail. "I could tell you were good people. And you know what. I'm going to give you a special rate on that AC unit. It normally costs $12,000 to put it in, I'll do it for $9,000. And that'll include the furnace."

"That, uh, sounds, very decent of you. It's a good price."

"Yeah, I try and help people where I can. That's the best price you'll find anywhere. I know you won't take title until next week, but we can get started tomorrow if you want, doing the ground work, pulling out that old furnace. I'll just need a deposit."

"How much?"

"I usually do 50 percent up front."

"That's a little steep," I said, trying to play this out realistically.

"Hey no prob. What works for you?"

"Hmm. maybe one-third? Maybe $3,000?"

"Sure," Billy said. "Let me go to my truck and write up the paperwork. I'll just need the deposit check."

I started to wonder if Juan's patrol officers would get here in time. I didn't have my checkbook on me and certainly wouldn't be giving any money to Billy Ray Fox. But I got the feeling if I didn't hand him something, Billy would leave and might never come back. Plus, he had George in tow. Taking on two potentially dangerous criminals didn't sound like a good plan with Gail standing nearby. Even with my .38 at the ready, too much could happen. But in an instant, everything changed.

With a start, the front door swung open. But instead of two uniformed LAPD officers entering, we stood face-to-face with Amanda Hertz. Her right arm was fully extended, and in her hand was a snub-nosed Ruger LCP pistol. It was the type of gun a woman might carry. It was small enough to have the appearance of being a toy but it was a gun, and a gun that could do some damage. Aimed at the right part of the body, it had the ability to kill someone, especially if it was fired at close range. And it was pointed straight at the chest of Billy the Fixer.

Sixteen

It was the third time this week that I found myself facing a person holding a gun. Things came in bunches all right, not all of them good. Everyone's eyes were on Amanda as her chest heaved unevenly and her hand appeared shaky. Her breathing was disjointed and her face radiated a toxic mix of fear and fury. She took a step forward, and instinctively, all of us took a step backwards. Billy continued moving until he was flush against a wall. George was closest to Amanda, a few feet to her right, and he seemed to be surveying just how close he really was.

"Finally ... finally found you," she said, seemingly gulping for some air. "You ... seemed to have dropped off the face of this, this earth."

Billy slowly shook his head. "Look, I tried calling you."

"No, no, you didn't," Amanda countered, her voice still shaky. "You're a liar. And a thief. And a ... a piece of shit."

"We can talk about this. I know you have to be upset. But I didn't mean to cause you any hurt. I swear, may the Lord be my witness ... "

"Shut up!" she screamed, and waved the weapon dangerously at Billy. "Lies! I don't want to hear any more lies!"

The room became silent once again. Amanda seemed to be trying to figure out her next move. Sometimes a person becomes so fixated on revenge, that when the opportunity finally comes to fruition, they momentarily lose the sense of what they had planned on doing. I watched George edge a small step closer to Amanda. Gail and I stood to her left.

"Amanda," I started, trying to draw her attention away from George. "The police will be here any minute. You can't go forward with this."

"No. The police won't come here."

I paused for a long second. "I called them a few minutes ago. They're on their way."

Amanda shook her head rapidly back and forth. "No. I papered over the address on the outside of the house. And I spray painted the numbers on the curb. The address is no longer visible from the street. They won't know we're in this house."

Another very long moment of silence passed before I spoke again.

"Why are you doing this?" I asked softly.

"I've been taken advantage of," she said testily.

"I understand. Totally. I do. But it's just money. Money can be replaced. Human life can't. Money can be paid back."

"I'm well aware of that," she said, still aiming the gun at Billy. George slid a little closer.

"What else did he do to you?" I asked. Part of me wanted to keep her talking. Part of me wanted to learn the answer myself.

"You want to tell him, Billy?" snarled Amanda. "Tell them. Go on."

Billy's face held a lack of expression that was unnerving. It was as if Amanda was holding nothing more potent than a cup of coffee. "We were just doing what people do. We gave in to the moment. I think it was just our own human weakness."

As placid as Billy's face was, Amanda's face was becoming more contorted with anger. "Is that what you call it, Billy? Or is that just your way of saying you took me against my will?"

Billy held up his palms. "I admit to my failings. But you were willing too. I know I was wrong. We were wrong. I'm ashamed. I'm ..."

"Stop it!" she screamed, tears now wetting her cheeks. "Stop the lies!"

"What do you want me to do?" Billy asked. "You already went and had the abortion. You went against my wishes. Not to mention against God's wishes. You took a human life. I'm sorry that I wasn't strong enough to persuade you not to. I'm sorry for everything, I really am. I want to make this right. I can ..."

"God damn it! Shut the fuck up!"

This would have definitely been a good time for Billy to quit talking. But like any snake oil salesman, his gift was his tongue, and in Billy's case, he thought it was his salvation. He continued to apologize and engage in Pollyanna chatter, pleadingly trying to invoke the name of God in a most generous way. And he was completely unaware of what he was about to set in motion.

Right at that moment, apparently at her breaking point, Amanda leaned forward and extended her arm as far as it would reach. It was as if she were trying to put the gun inside Billy's heart and break it in as harsh a way as hers had been broken.

But with her eyes filled with tears, and using a pistol that was not known for extreme accuracy, she fired the gun wildly in Billy's direction. The shot missed its mark and the bullet lodged into the wall directly behind him. George was now just a few feet from Amanda, and he charged her and tried to grab her arm. She pulled away from him and the two struggled. I started to move towards them but the gun went off once more. It did not appear to be aimed at anyone in particular. The gun simply fired randomly, the result of two people wrestling for control, and the trigger inadvertently pulled. But this time the shot did not come anywhere close to Billy Ray Fox who was moving swiftly to his right, along the wall. In what was a most horrible scenario, one that I could never have conjured up in a million years, the bullet was fired in a trajectory that sent it straight on a path towards Gail Pepper.

There are moments in life when time freezes. When you have no control over what's happening and you become subject to the whims of fate and destiny. There is no good reason as to why an involuntary gunshot goes where it goes. There is no explanation for why some people are magnets for tragedy and others are spared. The randomness of life is inexplicable to me. For some people, faith takes over and gives them a level of comfort. They think there is a grand plan and things are meant to be the way they are for a reason. But in the longest second of my life, the instant where everything would change dramatically, was now upon me. And as that bullet soared towards Gail, my heart stopped, my eyes bugged, and my soul prepared to leave me forever.

It was close. As close as a whisker perhaps. I thought for a second that I saw the bullet skim through some strands of Gail's hair, but that may have simply been her movement prompted by the sound of the shot. As the bullet flew by her, much too close for comfort, it smashed through a large window sending shards of glass flying all over the lawn. Gail stood there for a moment, mouth agape and then turned to see the damage to the window. And she saw what we all saw. The fleeting figure of Billy Ray Fox jumping through the shattered window, rolling to his feet and scampering across the lawn towards his truck.

I needed another moment to regain my bearings. The shock was still there, but so was a growing rage, cold and furious. George now had a solid grip on Amanda's arm and was trying to shake the gun from her hand. She squirmed one more time though, and started to dislodge herself. I moved a couple of steps towards them and positioned my right foot in front of her. I swung my right arm back and sprung towards Amanda. I unleashed a vicious back punch straight into the center of her face. The blow connected as solidly as any I had ever thrown, much harder than was necessary to disarm her. It was a punch that was intended to do a ferocious amount of damage.

Amanda's head snapped backwards and her feet came out from under her. Landing on her back, the gun skidded across the floor. I raced over to grab it, but there was no need for any urgency. Amanda screamed in pain and her hands covered her face. Blood was emanating quickly. She screamed again and then began shaking and rocking back and forth.

"What did you do?" she cried. "What did you do to me?"

I didn't bother to answer. My breathing was deep and rapid. I looked around wildly, but there was no other movement in the room. George and Gail stared at her.

"You don't know what he did!" Amanda screamed. "He violated me! He violated my life!"

I looked at her and finally found my voice. "Maybe he did," I said huskily. "But you were about to violate mine."

*

The short vacuum of silence that followed lasted for less than 30 seconds. Gail, George and I looked at each other, but said nothing. Amanda wept, quieter now, but aside from some deep breathing, no other sound permeated the room. It was as if we were waiting for the next shoe to drop, the next piece of the scene to play itself out. And it did happen. Just not inside the house.

We heard the sound of an ignition being turned over and an engine starting. A couple of quick pumps of the accelerator emitted a loud roar. A transmission was shifted and tires squealed. And almost as soon as the mechanical noise of a vehicle in motion began, it ended quickly. It ended with a very loud bang and with the jarring sound of crunching metal and shattering glass. The three of us looked at each other and then raced out the front door.

Billy Ray Fox had wasted no time in jumping into his pickup truck and trying to vacate the premises. He had gunned the engine and was starting to peel away. In a few seconds he would have been gone, and it would have become far more difficult to catch him. When a criminal senses the authorities are on his tail, he often goes underground and his movements become very hard to trace. People like Billy Ray Fox live on the margins of society, moving in and out of the world the rest of us inhabit. They grab what they can and then they disappear. So it was perhaps sheer luck, or maybe divine intervention as Billy might have said. But in the hectic process of trying to escape the clutches of Amanda Hertz, Billy the Fixer went and plowed his truck straight into an oncoming car. It was a black sedan with chrome trim. And as Juan Saavedra got out to survey the physical damage to his vehicle, he didn't look very happy. Not one bit.

The front end of Juan's car was banged up, but it looked repairable. The truck however appeared to be smashed beyond repair. The engine was badly damaged, and the hood was pushed up high and severely dented. The front windshield was cracked with a spider web-like design, the result of Billy's head vaulting directly into it. In the process of making his hasty departure, Billy of course failed to secure his seat belt. He lay motionless against the steering wheel, head bleeding, and a sick expression on his face.

Juan walked over to the driver's side door, peered in for a moment, and then removed his cell phone from his jacket. He placed a quick call and two minutes later the paramedics arrived. About 15 minutes after that, the first of seven patrol cars arrived on the scene. I put my arms around Gail.

"Are you okay?" I asked.

"No," she said, in a voice that was unnaturally high pitched.

"Pretty scary."

"I'm just glad it happened quickly. I didn't have time to be frightened."

"I hate to tell you this. But the bad part starts now. It's going to take a while to put something this traumatic behind you."

"How long does it take?"

I hugged her tighter and sighed. "It depends on the person. Sometimes it can take forever."

The paramedics on the scene tended to Billy first, he appeared to have a concussion. Amanda had what was most likely a broken jaw and a few missing teeth. Both were taken off to the jail wing of Cedars-Sinai Medical Center, hopefully with a floor or two separating them. Billy would be charged with multiple counts of grand theft and a parole violation. Amanda was actually facing the more severe charge, which would include attempted murder. And though I went to bat for George, no amount of persuasion would trump the fact that he was carrying a small bag of crystal meth in his back pocket, next to the box cutter. After a while, a pair of police tow trucks came and carted away Billy's truck and Juan's car. I decided it was time to approach Juan and try and make amends. If that were even possible.

"Can I offer you a ride home, Lieutenant?" I asked, in as humble a tone as I could muster.

"You can go kiss my ass, Burnside," Juan said, without any hint of humor.

"I, uh, guess I'm going to owe you a few favors."

"Oh I'd say that's accurate. I'm going to own you by the time this is through. I really ought to run you in and keep you there overnight for setting up this mess."

"You know, there were some positives that came out of this."

Juan cocked an eyebrow. "How's that?"

"Three criminals have been safely removed from the streets of Gotham City. And you got to make the collar on all three."

"Yeah. And one of these criminals would never have committed a crime if you hadn't set it up and made it easy."

I shrugged and raised my palms. "There's only so much I can do, Juan."

"Did you have any suspicion she was going to pull something like this?"

I looked skyward and thought about it for a second too long.

"Yeah," Juan said. "That's what I figured."

"I warned her not to take matters into her own hands," I pointed out. "She didn't tell me about a sexual assault. She could have filed charges and probably would have gotten more attention than by pursuing fraud."

Gail was standing a few feet away. She walked over and spoke quietly. "Once she let us in, Burnside ordered Amanda to leave."

I nodded. "Who could have imagined she'd come back with a loaded gun?"

"You must have had some suspicions about her, I know you." Juan said. "But I have to question why you'd even bring your girlfriend along on this adventure."

I didn't have a good answer for that one. It was a question I'd be torturing myself over for a long time. "We all have regrets about things."

"It's not his fault, Lieutenant," Gail said, her voice still quiet and serious. "I wanted to come. And I have experience as a security officer. We had no idea it could possibly turn out like this. If anything, it was Billy Ray Fox who was the concern."

Juan looked at her and sighed. "Look, it's getting late. We'll finish up here. But I want to be clear. Don't pull this type of stunt again."

"No worries," I said, sensing Juan was softening.

"So I guess I'm going to see you at the game tomorrow," Juan managed.

"You certainly will."

"Yeah, you were a little vague on where you were sitting."

"That's true. I'm not sitting anywhere. I'm going to be on the sideline."

Juan stared at me. "Sideline passes?"

"Better than that. I'm leading the USC football team out on the field. I'm honorary captain for the game."

"Well," Juan said, digesting all this and not responding for a moment. "I guess it's a good thing for UCLA that I'm letting you go."

*

Gail and I spent a quiet Friday evening at home. We didn't say a lot, but held each other most of the time. I made a few resolutions that night, one of which was to never again involve her in one of my investigations. Curiosity and the cat. Gail was too important to me. I wasn't taking any more chances.

I slept fitfully, my mind kicking me awake a number of times. I couldn't remember any dreams, but the real life nightmare-that-almost-was kept playing in my mind. And I needed to come to grips with that thing I had been thinking and feeling for quite a while.

Ms. Linzmeier woke me early with her pulsating aerobics program. If she was up, I was up. Moving into the kitchen, I began the process of brewing a pot of French roast coffee, extra strong. Just as the first cup had finished drizzling its way into the decanter, my phone buzzed. The incoming phone number had a 702 area code. I had a hunch I knew who was calling.

"Detective Chandler," I said. "You're up early."

"As are you, pal. Got some good news for you."

"I'm always into hearing good news."

"That fellow you were asking about the other day, that Adam Barber. He was picked up at McCarran Airport last night. Had a satchel with $800,000 in cash, headed to Switzerland. Non-stop flight to Geneva, if I recall correctly."

I laughed. "No law against leaving Las Vegas with a boatload of money is there? Unless the IRS took notice."

"Ha!" Chandler laughed. "Looks like his luck ran out. He was traveling with this couple, man and a woman, each of them had over $2 million in cash themselves. There was a warrant out for them for embezzlement, wire fraud, a few other things. They'll probably add tax evasion to the list. Looks like your man Barber was traveling with the wrong companions, that's how we got him. But for this Barber guy, we've got an extra special charge lined up."

"What's that?"

"Murder. The idiot checked a bag with a handgun in it. Turns out that was the same gun used to shoot Henry Simon, that security guard that bought it last week."

"Taking a gun overseas. No one ever said crooks were smart."

"Yeah. Just when you think you've seen everything. Anyways, when the name Adam Barber popped up, I recognized it and figured you'd want to know."

"Absolutely, I'm very glad you called. And the smart money says his two companions were named Isabelle Larson and Glen Butterworth."

"Winner," he replied. "The funny thing was the charges were apparently filed in Los Angeles by a family member. Someone named Clara Larson. And she had a hunch they'd be leaving out of Vegas. Interesting world they must live in."

Interesting barely scratched the surface of that one. I thanked Detective Chandler for the news. Apparently Clara had wasted no time in taking steps to rebuild her life. Doing so meant taking down her daughter. It was a price she seemed to have no problem paying. I took Gail through what had happened and she listened quietly and intently. We both agreed that the Larsons were as dysfunctional a family as had ever been thrown together. And we also agreed that this didn't have to be the case. It could easily have been different. Most families were.

We left soon after for the Coliseum. It was still early in the morning, but our leaving now was not just to beat traffic or to get a parking space. For the first time in over 20 years, my presence was required in the Trojan locker room. My eyes were wide with delight, and I was going to enjoy this day. The weather was perfect for football, the type of day an athlete prays for. The sky was a bright blue and there were a series of high, skeletal clouds. They formed a quilted pattern which indicated rain soon, but not for another day or so. The temperature was cool for the region, maybe in the low 60s, with hardly any breeze. I had a good feeling about today. In a lot of ways.

I didn't speak to the team before the game, that was the job of Johnny Cleary and he gave an inspired pre-game pep talk. By the time he was done, I was ready to put on a helmet and pads myself. Along with the team captains, I led close to 100 players through the Coliseum tunnel. A crowd of over 90,000 fans stood cheering as we poured onto the field. It was a sellout, which was not unusual. Having two nationally ranked college football teams in the same state was unusual. Having them in the same city, separated by all of 10 miles was as unique as could be. USC-UCLA was a football game unlike any other.

The two universities recruited the same football players, played in the same conference against the same schools and monitored each other carefully throughout the season. At one time the L.A. Coliseum -- site of the 1932 and 1984 Summer Olympic games -- was home for both teams, despite the fact that the stadium was practically in USC's back yard. And when the two schools played each other each year, both wore their home uniforms, the Trojans in cardinal jerseys, the Bruins in powder blue.

Even after UCLA moved its home games to Pasadena in the early 1980s, the tradition of both teams wearing their home-colored jerseys continued for a while. Then an NCAA statute was passed for college football, requiring the visiting team to always wear white. This was a silly legacy dating back to an era when many people had black-and-white TVs in their homes and they needed a way to distinguish the two teams. But the light blue shade of UCLA's uniforms contrasted enough with USC's darker jerseys to give viewers a clear opportunity to tell who was who.

It was many years before a solution was reached that allowed both teams to wear their colors at the same time. The first time this happened was on UCLA's home turf in 2008. When the teams ran out on the field, the officials immediately threw a penalty flag on USC for not wearing white jerseys. The referees penalized them and took away one of their three time-outs for the first half. In a supportive gesture, UCLA immediately called time out, to prevent one team from having an undue advantage. It was a fine demonstration of sportsmanship. The tradition continued for a couple of years that way, with the home team returning the favor and burning a time-out to keep things even. This required a sense of trust and honesty, something both schools maintained in earnest.

Finally, as a direct result of what USC and UCLA were doing, the NCAA came to its senses and eliminated the penalty on visiting teams for wearing colored jerseys. And while UCLA would occasionally wear white when they came to the Coliseum, today they were decked out in their blue and gold, the blue jerseys having become a little darker over the years. As I ran out onto the Coliseum turf for the first time in over two decades, I couldn't help but think of how we'd all changed quite a bit over the years.

I went over and shook hands with the UCLA head coach, and even got to participate in the traditional mid-field coin toss to start the game. We won the toss and Johnny told the team captains to defer receiving the kickoff until the second half, a decision that would have huge ramifications on the outcome of the game. I returned to the sideline where I was joined by Gail. We wore our sideline passes proudly, and enjoyed the sights and sounds that can only come from being right next to the players.

USC kicked off to start the game, and UCLA responded by immediately returning the kick up the sideline for 90 yards, before the Trojan kicker was able to wrestle the UCLA ball carrier to the ground. This being a USC home game, the crowd was primarily comprised of USC fans, but there was still a large UCLA contingent in attendance. The Bruin fans roared, but their thrill ride was short-lived. The Trojan defense stiffened and UCLA settled for a field goal to go up 3-0.

The first half was mostly a cautious tale of short passes and interior running plays. It was reminiscent of a boxing match where the two fighters keep feeling each other out, each one looking for a chink in the other's armor. Finding little, both teams took calculated shots, but the main goal was to avoid making a mistake. Marcellus Williams caught a couple of passes, but was essentially bottled up by a UCLA defense that shadowed him closely the entire half. At one point UCLA fumbled on their own 30-yard line and the Trojans moved the ball close to the end zone, but ultimately had to settle for a field goal. At the end of the first half, the score was tied 3-3.

Gail and I stayed on the field during halftime and enjoyed watching the marching bands from the two schools perform. The Trojan band had a larger contingent, and when spread out, they covered the field from goal line to goal line. After about 20 minutes, the teams returned from their respective locker rooms. As USC lined up to receive the second-half kickoff, I noticed the hint of a smile on Johnny Cleary's face. I also noticed the same look on the face of Marcellus Williams.

We were standing near the closed end of the Coliseum, and the Bruins kicked off the other way. The ball floated just past the goal line near the peristyle end which featured colonnade arches, supporting the Olympic cauldron torch in the center. The Trojan kick returner fielded the ball one yard deep in the end zone and then went down on one knee, signaling a touchback that would bring the ball out to the 25-yard line.

"Strange," I commented. "We usually run those kicks out of the end zone."

Gail nodded, but said nothing. She was still learning the game and I think she just enjoyed being on the sideline with me on such a beautiful day. And the fact that whatever mayhem was happening around us was controlled and legal.

USC's offense moved quickly onto the field and lined up without a huddle. The UCLA defense looked around in confusion and began to get mildly panicked by what they saw. The Trojans lined up in a no-back formation, with four wide receivers lined up bunched to the left side. The Bruins scrambled around before both safeties and a linebacker scurried over to where a lone cornerback had been positioned to try and defend whatever Johnny Cleary had up his sleeve.

The quarterback took the snap and three of the receivers shot forward as blockers, knocking down the safeties and causing two other defenders to trip over themselves. One of the wide receivers moved two steps backwards and the quarterback then threw a bullet pass directly to him. With the three other receivers serving as blockers, a clear path had been forged. The Trojans were executing a bubble screen, UCLA was thrown completely off guard, and Marcellus Williams had the ball. There was only one defender in front of him.

The beauty of the bubble screen is that the formation makes it look like the offense is setting up for a normal downfield pass. But instead, the quarterback quickly throws the ball laterally and gets it in the hands of a specific wide receiver, while the other receivers block for him. It effectively turns the wide receiver into a running back, something unexpected. The exceptional receivers can then use their speed and agility to move forward in a manner they don't always have the opportunity to employ. The downsides are big, though. If a bubble screen pass is intercepted, the defender can usually just waltz into the end zone for a defensive touchdown, because there is no one in his path. High risk, high reward.

Marcellus caught the pass and quickly cut to his right, past the gaggle of Bruin defenders being overpowered by the three receivers. The one defender in his path was a linebacker. Marcellus put a juke move on him, bobbing his head and dancing back and forth very quickly. Unable to keep up, the linebacker simply lost his balance and fell to the ground. Marcellus ran by him, never touching the defender, it was all shuck and jive. In athletic parlance, Marcellus broke the other guy's ankles, because it looked like he couldn't stand and he just fell over. And with that, Marcellus Williams was on his way to the end zone 75 yards away. A linebacker tried to move over and dive at Marcellus' legs, but he was too late. There is nothing worse than being too late. No one was in front of Marcellus and no one was going to catch him.

Great athletes have what is sometimes referred to as an extra gear. When they need to outrun someone, they dig down and accelerate at a pace beyond their normal stride. Their fast-twitch muscle fibers are properly conditioned to allow them to build speed in short distances. And that was exactly what Marcellus was doing. His legs were simply moving up and down faster than anyone else's. A pair of UCLA defenders chased him for about 50 yards before slowing down and finally stopping, their hands on their hips in frustration. From their perspective, Marcellus had become a blur. Nothing but tail lights.

From where we were standing, Marcellus was practically running right at us. And as he passed us by, running full tilt, I could have sworn I saw a smile breaking through his lips, a shine of delight in his eyes, and an expression of unmitigated joy. He looked up at the Jumbotron near the top of the Coliseum. The huge HD screen's primary purpose was to give fans a greater view of the game. But it also served to give players something of a rear-view mirror to see who was behind them, and just how far back they were. When

Marcellus looked skywards at the Jumbotron he saw just how much distance he had on the defenders. And as they slowed down, he slowed down, too.

At the 5-yard line, Marcellus turned around and backpedaled into the end zone, high-stepping, and holding the ball out at the defenders in a mixture of taunting and defiance. The ref threw a penalty flag for unsportsmanlike conduct, but it would matter not. Marcellus tore off his helmet and danced around the end zone, fist pumping, exhorting the wildly jubilant crowd into even more histrionics. His teammates finally caught up with him in the end zone and mobbed him. The entire Trojan bench was going crazy, jumping up and down, and the partisan USC crowd was as vocal as could be. Even the air felt like it was shaking. The extra point made it 10-3, and the tide had turned.

Over the next 17 minutes, USC rained five more touchdowns down on UCLA, with two of these going to Marcellus, giving him three TDs for the day. By the time they were done, the score was 45-3 and some fans, mostly UCLA's, had already begun exiting the Coliseum. With most of the 4th quarter left, Johnny began to insert some of the backups and walk-ons, the guys who had contributed mightily in the team's practice and preparation, but rarely ever got to play in a game. The match ended without any more scoring, but the rout had been administered.

As the clock went to 0:00, I approached Marcellus to high-five him, but he gave me a big bear hug instead. He also hugged Gail, which I'm sure she enjoyed more than I did a few feet away. I found Johnny and congratulated him. The fans had poured onto the field and started dancing on the Coliseum field. The Trojan band began to play and some of the players took turns climbing a stepladder, grabbing the ceremonial sword and conducting the band. When it was Marcellus' turn, he climbed to the very top of the ladder and lifted the sword high in the air, leading an inspired version of "Fight On."

Gail and I watched the festivities and then I walked her over to the peristyle end of the Coliseum. The Olympic cauldron torch above us, was lit as it always was during the fourth quarter of Trojan football games. It was a bright, burning reminder of the Coliseum's heritage as the host for two separate Olympiads. And I was going to make it even more memorable for us.

I took Gail's hand, smiled, and then nervously bent down on one knee. In the background the band and crowd began to spell out USC's SO-CAL cheer.

"S-O-U-T!" they yelled.

"I've been thinking a lot about us," I began, raising my voice so she could hear me.

Gail looked at me and said nothing, but I noticed her gray eyes widening.

"I have to have you in my life. There's no other option."

"Oh my. Is this going where I think it's going?"

"H-E-R-N!" the crowd chanted loudly.

Behind us, two guys with a video camera and boom approached us. "Can we record this?!" they asked, screaming to be heard.

Gail and I looked at each other and smiled at the same time.

"What do you think?" she asked me.

"Why not?" I yelled hoarsely, and turned to them. "Go ahead!"

"C-A-L-I!"

"I don't think I can live without you," I managed, suddenly having some trouble speaking.

"I don't think I can live without you, either," Gail answered, her voice not containing the least bit of hesitation.

"So will you do me the honor ... " I gulped.

"F-O-R-N-I-A!

I took a very deep breath and let the words spill out loudly. ".... of marrying me?!"

Gail pulled me to my feet and wrapped her arms tightly around my neck.

"SOUTHERN! CALIFO-RRRRRRRRR-NIA!!!"

Though the crowd was roaring, I could hear Gail perfectly as she whispered in my ear, the words I'd been dying to hear, but scared to death of hearing. And in the whirring, frenetic pace of a single moment, my world came together, and everything suddenly aligned perfectly.

"Of course I will, honey," she whispered, in the sweetest voice I had ever heard, in a timbre that was decisive and final and crystal clear. "In fact, I thought you'd never ask."

The End

About The Author

David Chill was born and raised in New York City and educated in the public schools. After receiving his undergraduate degree from SUNY-Oswego, he moved to Los Angeles where he earned a Masters degree from the University of Southern California. David Chill is the author of four novels: Post Pattern, Fade Route, Bubble Screen and Safety Valve, all featuring Burnside, a private investigator and former LAPD officer and college football star.

Post Pattern was a finalist in the St. Martin's Press contest for New Private Eye Mystery Writers. Both Post Pattern and Fade Route have received critical acclaim, and both have spent time on the Amazon.com best seller lists. David Chill currently lives in Los Angeles with his wife and son. If you wish to contact David Chill directly, please email him at: davidchill3214@gmail.com

If you enjoyed Bubble Screen, then don't miss David Chill's fourth Burnside novel....

Safety Valve

Here is a sample of this terrific new mystery...

SAFETY VALVE PREVIEW

Cliff Roper was someone I hoped I would never see again. He had been arrested numerous times, he had an obnoxious personality, and he possessed a manner that could easily engender distrust. But when Cliff Roper was suspected of trying to kill his business partner, the calculus changed. He arrived at my office with $10,000 in cash, something that was enough to make me reconsider my hastily formed opinion.

"You gotta help me," he said.

"I don't gotta do anything," I countered, wondering why my command of the English language had suddenly disappeared.

"I'll pay you a month's wages."

"I charge a thousand dollars a day," I informed him, suddenly raising my daily rate to factor in some combat pay that might make him re-consider this case.

"You're kidding me."

"I don't kid about money."

"Crap," he said, as the wheels inside of his head seemed to turn furiously. "Make it two weeks."

"I haven't even decided to accept you as a client yet."

"Oh, you're going to decide? Like hell you will. I'm the decider here, Burnside. The client gets to choose. I know that from personal experience."

Perhaps he did. A small, wiry man with close cropped

silver hair, Cliff Roper was a successful sports agent. He represented athletes in nearly every sport you could think of, and possibly a few you couldn't. He was well dressed, sporting a grey blazer and slacks, and wore a white oxford cloth shirt with the first three buttons open.

Despite the debonair look, Cliff Roper was someone well acquainted with the inside of a jail cell. He had been detained numerous times for everything from embezzlement to manslaughter, although none of the charges ever turned into a conviction. He was tough, savvy, intense, and rich. He was also the type with which I did not normally associate. The thought of doing business with him made me more than a little apprehensive.

"If I recall, you once threatened to have me killed," I said.

"And If I recall," he countered evenly, "you threatened me with blackmail. Sounds like we're even."

"Even?"

"More or less. Look, why don't we just try and put all that stuff behind us. I need someone like you."

I took a deep breath. Business had been very slow lately and with an upcoming wedding to pay for, not to mention my monthly bills, I decided I had an obligation to at least hear him out.

"Why don't you start by telling me what brings you here," I said.

"Someone's trying to frame me," he declared.

"For what?"

"For what? For attempted murder is for what."

"Who'd you try to kill? Allegedly, of course." I asked.

"I didn't try to kill anyone. That's the point. Geez. Do I have to spell it out for you?"

"Yes. And start from the beginning. It'll make things easier. At least for me."

Cliff Roper took a big, long sigh and looked out my window for a moment. I doubt he saw anything more than a smoggy morning in April. The winter rains that roared through southern California had ended for the season. Without them, the air had begun to grow stale and ugly again. Some diffuse sunlight was starting to emerge from the thicket in the sky.

"I have this partner," Roper said. "Or former partner as of last week. Name is Gilbert Horn. We've been running a sports agency for a couple of years now. But I'm the only one bringing in new clients and he's the only one losing existing ones. It's not a good balance."

"So you split up."

"Yeah, yeah, we split up. Or more to the point I told him to take a hike, because he wasn't holding up his end. He didn't like that too much. He made some threats."

"What were the threats?"

"Ah, the usual. He'd sue me, bankrupt me, ruin me. Chop me into little pieces."

"I see. The usual."

"Right," he agreed enthusiastically, pleased I was able to grasp his point. "I told him to get lost. I've been threatened by guys a lot tougher than him."

"Then what?'

"Then last week my office gets burglarized. Someone cracked the safe. I don't keep a lot there, but they took some emergency cash, a few contracts. And they also took my Glock."

"Your gun?" I peered at him, assuming he was referring to a Glock automatic pistol.

"Yeah, yeah, my gun. It was a Glock 34 if you want to get technical."

"You kept it in the safe."

"Look, I'm not Wyatt Earp. I don't normally walk around carrying a heater."

"And you think your partner took it."

"He's the only one who could have figured out the combination. Or stolen it. Anyway, what happened next is where it gets weird."

"So *now* it's getting weird?" I asked, my eyebrows shooting up involuntarily. I was glad I didn't have anything else to do this morning. Cliff Roper had, if nothing else, high entertainment value.

"Yeah," he continued. "Someone took a couple of shots at my business partner the other night. Outside his own home. Didn't hit him but the shots lodged into the outside wall of his house."

"And he thinks it was you."

"It's worse. The police do too."

"Where does he live?"

"Lookout Mountain. Off of Laurel Canyon. Not far from where I live."

"Hollywood Hills," I said.

"Yeah. Close to my office. And I don't need to tell you this, but it's a rotten time for me to have a problem with the law. The NFL draft is next week. I got a lot on the line. Got a couple of college guys that could get picked early. That's big money on the table."

"Your partner sign any college players?"

Roper scoffed. "Just one. Some running back out of Buttcrack State. Gil said he was clocked at a 4.3 in the 40."

"That's pretty darned fast. Close to Olympic levels."

"It's bull. He was clocked on his pro day at his college. And that college has a track that slopes downward. Everyone in the business knows that players' times there are artificially lower. That is everyone who pays attention. My numb nuts ex-partner didn't even know this. He even loaned the kid five large to get him to sign with our agency."

I shook my head. A loan of five thousand dollars is tantamount to a bribe. In the agent world though, that's sometimes the price of doing business.

Roper sensed my disapproval. "You want guys to sign with you? It's a difference maker."

I rubbed the bridge of my nose and tried to get his attention focused once more on the shooting. A few things didn't quite add up here. "So let's go back to the other day. The bullets they found were from a Glock."

"You're a genius. Just like the cops. Only thing is, I didn't have my gun. It was stolen, remember?"

"You file a police report on the burglary?" I asked.

"I don't do that sort of thing."

"Of course you don't," I said. "Because that would be a matter of public record. And it would alert your existing clients and maybe make them a little nervous about who's representing them."

Roper nodded slowly as he looked at me. "I knew you

weren't stupid."

"And I know that too," I responded sharply. "The larger question is are you stupid?"

"Me?" he asked, the shocked look on his face was far from feigned. I didn't imagine Cliff Roper had ever doubted himself in his life. "How'd you wind up there?"

"Someone stole your pistol. They had plans for it, most likely of a criminal nature. You don't report the theft. The gun gets used in a crime. It's fired at someone so it's attempted murder. They tie it back to you. In the eyes of the police, you're now a person of interest."

Roper slumped back in his chair. It was hardly a soft chair, but Roper wasn't a soft man. He rubbed the bridge of his nose and his mouth contorted into an ugly expression. He did not strike me as a man who liked to be toyed with, and I could only imagine the revenge he was cooking up in his head.

"Okay," he said, finally. "You got me."

"Let me ask you this. Who filed the police report regarding the shooting?"

"Horn's wife. Said her husband was in hiding now. He knows someone wants him dead."

"Did she identify you?"

"I don't know what that crazy broad said. She's a gold digger. Anything that comes out of her mouth is designed to put money in her pocket or diamonds on her body."

"And the police questioned you when?"

"Last night."

"You have an alibi for where you were yesterday?"

"Don't worry," he said, dismissing the concern with a

wave of his hand. "I arranged for one."

"Wonderful," I said. Clients like Cliff Roper were a double edged sword. They paid a lot of money, but were high maintenance and they were flexible with the truth. It was nothing more than a tactic to get them past obstacles. They were untrustworthy and secretive and they wasted a lot of a private investigator's time because they withheld certain facts and details which they didn't feel like sharing. But they are often willing to pay a boatload of money, so we sometimes take on their cases. I suppose that's why they call what we do "work."

"Let me ask you this," I continued. "Who do *you* think fired the shot at Horn?"

Roper emitted a laugh that had a sneer hanging from the end of it. "I can give you a long list."

"Let's start with a short one."

"Okay. For starters, there are a couple of clients who'd like to put his head through a wall. He messed up Oscar Romeo's endorsement deal with a sneaker company. Horn didn't follow through on the details, didn't present the client in the proper light. Cost Oscar $3 million, so he dumped us. Then there's Oscar's pal, Patrick Washington. The two have been friends forever. The Raiders sent Patrick a 5-year renewal contract, fully guaranteed. It just had to be signed and faxed back by midnight at the end of March. Patrick signed it, but Horn the dimwit, he couldn't figure out how to work the fax machine because his assistant wasn't working that night. The schmuck never heard of Kinko's? Or Staples? So Patrick has to go the free agent route and his new agent still doesn't have a deal for him yet. Horn was asleep at the wheel. You can't operate like that in this business."

I had heard about both of them. Romeo and Washington grew up here in Los Angeles, although both played college football elsewhere. The southern California region was rich with talented prospects. Along with Texas and Florida, it was prime recruiting ground for every college football coach in America. The guys who did well in High School were offered scholarships to colleges all over the country. They sometimes made it to the pro ranks, but many still returned to make L.A. their home in the off-season.

"Who else?"

"That's not enough for you to start with?"

"It is. I just like to be thorough."

Roper processed this for a minute. "There's Brendon Webster."

"The name sounds familiar."

"It should. He was a 5-star recruit out of Huntington Beach. Played defensive tackle at Texas A&M for three years. Was all set to go pro after his junior year. Then he got his knee torn up in a bowl game. Never recovered. Works as a leg breaker now. How's that for karma?"

"Who does he work for?"

Roper hesitated. "Couple of former associates. Let's leave it at that."

"I take it Brendon didn't stay at A&M to get his degree."

"You kidding? He had an I.Q. that was in double digits. Guy couldn't spell dog if you spotted him the 'd' and the 'o' for crissakes. We fed him the answers to the Wonderlic test and he still got most of the questions wrong."

"Tough break for him, especially if football was all he

could do. You know, that's how my football career as a safety ended. Knee injury. I was a four year starter at USC. Only difference was I ended up in law enforcement. Sounds like Brendon ended up on the other side of the fence."

Roper shrugged. "You're all part of the same sewer system. You just operate on different sides."

"Thanks. You have a nice way of putting things. Anyone else a possibility?"

"Look, Horn just got kicked out of his agency, he lost most of his clients, and his other investments are tanking. The list can be as long as you want it to be. There's no shortage of people who might have wanted to take a pop at him."

"Investments?" I asked. "What investments are tanking?"

"Yeah, I forgot about that. He's part owner of a car dealership in Santa Monica. Luxury imports. Did well at first, but the recession took a lot of money off the table. Heard things aren't going so well there."

"Guy sounds like he's got a lot of problems. Maybe contributed to his under-performing on the job?"

"Yeah, sure, whatever. But I don't care about excuses. I got a business to run. I can't carry dead weight."

"Of course not," I said. "What about women?"

"What about them?"

"You said he was married. He have a girlfriend on the side?"

"Sure. Who doesn't?"

I rubbed the bridge of my nose. "Go on."

"So he had a few girlfriends on the side. I don't know

them personally. But I also don't know why they would take a shot at him. His wife, maybe. But not them."

"Sometimes the girlfriend is led to believe the guy will leave his wife."

"No," he said, feigning disbelief. "You think?"

I did my best to ignore his grating personality. It wasn't easy. Part of me wanted to throw him out of my office. Part of me needed the money. And a part of me was intrigued with this case.

"So you haven't brought up Horn's wife as a possibility," I pointed out. "When a violent act occurs, the spouse is normally the first suspect."

"April? I dunno. If she knew his financial situation was dire, then no. Why kill a drowning man? I don't know what motive she'd have. Besides, she was right next to him when the shot was fired."

"Okay," I said, trying to process all of this. "I think I have enough info to get started."

"Then we're done here."

"Not quite," I said, thinking about the type of individual with whom I was about to become involved. The ethical side of me said to walk away from this case. The practical side of me said to take the money. The investigator in me was intrigued and that was usually the determining factor.

"I'll need a retainer before I begin. And I think two weeks should work."

He gave me a sharp look. "Paying one large a day is a lot of money."

"It is. But I'm good and I think you know that I'm good. I'll do everything I can to find out who did this," I said, hoping that the culprit wasn't Roper himself. "You'll get your money's worth. That's the one thing I can promise you."

"This your only case?"

"I've got one other," I said, thinking about the home insurance fraud I needed to follow up on. "But yours is the one that's most pressing, and yours will come first. I'll work on the other when time permits."

Roper looked out the window for a long moment before turning back to me. "You were asking about his wife and girlfriends. How about you. Are you married?"

"Engaged," I said. "Wedding's in a month."

"First time at the plate?"

"That's right."

"I've struck out four times. Would've been five, but the first one got annulled. She was underage."

"I'm planning on mine lasting forever."

"Yeah," he said, opening up a satchel filled with hundred dollar bills and dumping them on my desk. "That's what they all think."

*

To purchase the full copy of Safety Valve, visit Amazon.com

Bubble Screen

David Chill

www.ingramcontent.com/pod-product-compliance
Lightning Source LLC
Chambersburg PA
CBHW020618260626
47157CB00003B/1071